"Well, the proverbial bad penny has turned up once more."

Vincenzo seemed to recover his composure instantly and stood looking down at Leah with eyes like black cinders.

"And what, might I ask, are you doing here?" she demanded stiffly.

"The same as you, I imagine. Looking for the lovebirds. But we're both too late. The lovebirds have flown." He leaned against the doorjamb, exuding from every taut, hard sinew the same smoldering arrogance that she remembered so well.

Leah stepped forward and frowned at him. "What do you mean, 'flown'? Would you mind telling me where my sister's gone."

Vincenzo didn't answer her. Instead, he accused her, "Was it you who put your sister up to this game she's playing? Was it your idea that she come to Rome and start flirting with my sister's son?"

Stephanie Howard is a British author whose two ambitions since childhood were to see the world and to write. Her first venture into the world was a four-year stay in Italy, learning the language and supporting herself by writing short stories. Then her sensible side brought her back to London to study Social Administrations at the London School of Economics. She has held various editorial posts at magazines such as *Reader's Digest, Vanity Fair,* and *Women's Own.* She has also written free-lance for *Cosmopolitan, Good Housekeeping* and the *Observer.*

Books by Stephanie Howard

HARLEQUIN ROMANCE

3093—MASTER OF GLEN CRANNACH
3112—AN IMPOSSIBLE PASSION
3153—WICKED DECEIVER
3195—ROMANTIC JOURNEY
3220—A MATTER OF HONOUR
3237—DANGEROUS INFATUATION

HARLEQUIN PRESENTS

1098—RELUCTANT PRISONER
1130—DARK LUCIFER
1168—HIGHLAND TURMOIL
1273—BRIDE FOR A PRICE
1307—KISS OF THE FALCON
1450—A BRIDE FOR STRATHALLANE

A ROMAN MARRIAGE
Stephanie Howard

Harlequin Books

TORONTO • NEW YORK • LONDON
AMSTERDAM • PARIS • SYDNEY • HAMBURG
STOCKHOLM • ATHENS • TOKYO • MILAN
MADRID • WARSAW • BUDAPEST • AUCKLAND

Original hardcover edition published in 1992
by Mills & Boon Limited

ISBN 0-373-03247-1

Harlequin Romance first edition February 1993

A ROMAN MARRIAGE

CHAPTER ONE

So FAR, so good, Leah congratulated herself privately, as she made her way along the busy Via del Corso, hurrying in spite of the fierce August heat. She had been in Rome now for all of twelve hours and the thing she had feared most, mercifully, hadn't happened. She had not come face to face with Vincenzo.

Yet his shadow was everywhere, she thought with a small shiver. On this street where they had walked together so often all those years ago, in the buildings that surrounded her, in the very air she breathed.

She shook herself inwardly. Stop it, she chided herself. To think of Vincenzo was to awaken painful memories, and she had enough on her mind without stirring up the past.

With a determined frown, Leah shook back her hair, a glistening waterfall of palest golden brown that fell past her shoulders and swung softly as she walked. And she clenched her fists and straightened her spine beneath the soft blue cotton shirtdress she wore. She had come here for Jo's sake and that was all she must think of. She had to stop her little sister from ruining her life.

For a moment she paused to look around her and squint down at the slip of paper in her hand. The little side-street where Jo's flat was located, she had been quite certain, was somewhere near here.

'*Posso auitare?*' Can I help? At once, a passer-by was offering assistance.

Leah smiled at him gratefully. '*Sto cercando questa strada.*' She held out the piece of paper with the address.

'*E là, a sinistra.*' It's there on the left. The man nodded and pointed to the narrow turning just ahead of them.

Leah thanked him. '*Grazie.*' So, she had been right, after all! And she smiled a rueful smile to herself. It was five years since she had last set foot in Rome, yet her knowledge of the city had instantly come back to her, as had her knowledge of the language.

She felt a flutter of emotion squeeze deep within her. It was all so familiar, yet now so painfully alien.

Dismissing the thought, she turned up the little side-street and forced herself to focus on the task ahead. It wouldn't be easy. Her sister was headstrong—quite as headstrong as Leah had been at her age. But she had to convince her that she was heading for disaster. She had to stop her from repeating her own fatal mistake.

She found the building she was looking for—an old stone-fronted apartment block—and pushed open the front door that was standing ajar.

Flat six, third floor. She strode across the hall, past the empty porter's cubby-hole in one corner, and headed swiftly for the stairs, silently praying that Jo was at home. There had been no reply when she had phoned yesterday evening, nor when she had tried again a couple of times this morning. She crossed her fingers. She *had* to talk to her.

A little breathless she reached the third floor and strode to the door with the big brass '6'. 'OK. Here goes.' She jabbed the doorbell. 'Please be in,' she muttered to herself.

Not a sound was to be heard from inside the flat. Leah felt her spirits sink a little. But a moment later, as she was about to ring again, to her delight she heard the sound of footsteps.

She sighed with relief and smiled in anticipation, as the latch on the other side was quickly pulled back. Then a moment later the door swung open and the ground seemed to fall away beneath her feet as she found herself looking into the harsh dark face of the man she had prayed never to set eyes on again.

Leah could not speak. It was like an emotional earthquake. In one explosive instant five years had crumbled.

'Well, look who it is! The proverbial bad penny, finally turned up again after all these years.'

Vincenzo had recovered his composure instantly and stood now looking down at her with eyes like black cinders. He still hated her, Leah thought, feeling a chill ripple through her, just as fiercely as she still hated him.

Through the fog in her head she demanded stiffly, 'And what, might I ask, are you doing here?'

'The same as you, I imagine. Looking for the lovebirds. But we're both too late. The lovebirds have flown.'

He was standing in the doorway, leaning against the door-jamb, exuding from every taut hard sinew the same smouldering arrogance that she remembered so well.

He hasn't changed, Leah thought with satisfaction, as she looked into his face with its hard
bold lines, the eyes as black as jet, the curved bony
nose, the wide mouth set in a cold cynical line. In
five and half years she had thought he might have
softened. But a hunk of granite didn't soften.
Thank heavens, she thought gratefully, that I left
when I did.

At the thought she felt the tension inside her
slacken, as though she had overcome some crucial
hurdle. And suddenly she was glad she had come
face to face with him. Finally, in her heart, she knew
she could handle it.

She stepped forward and frowned at him. 'What
do you mean, "flown"? Would you mind telling
me where my sister's gone?'

Vincenzo did not answer her. Instead, he accused her, 'Was it you who put your sister up to
this game she's playing? Was it your idea that she
come to Rome and start messing around with my
sister's son?'

Perish the thought! 'It most certainly was not!
The last thing I'd want for anyone I love is to get
mixed up with a member of your family!' Wasn't
that why she was here—to put an end to the romance that Jo had told her about in her letters?

But Vincenzo wasn't listening. 'What did you
hope to get out of it? Was it just to annoy me, or
did you have some other motive?'

'I had nothing to do with it! Nothing whatsoever! If you want to know the truth, if I'd had
my way, Jo would never even have set foot in
Rome!'

'And why did *you* come? To egg her on? To make sure she does a thorough job of first leading on and then screwing up poor Carlo? Were you planning to give her a few sisterly tips? After all, you're the expert in that department!'

'Me? Don't be so modest! *You're* the expert! When it comes to screwing people up in the name of romance, believe me, there's nobody who can touch you!'

As she glared into his face, raw emotion burning through her, Leah was suddenly aware that this bitter little scene was like a carbon copy of all those other countless scenes that had once torn her apart all those long years ago.

She took a step back and quickly caught her breath, hating the way her limbs were shaking. 'I didn't come here to fight.' She glared hard at him. 'I came to find Jo. Kindly tell me where she is.'

But he was turning away sharply, stepping back into the apartment. 'Go on, get out of here! Go back to England. One damned female member of your family stirring up trouble here is already quite enough!'

He was about to close the door, but she stepped forward quickly. 'Tell me where my sister is and I'll take her back with me. That's what I came here to do anyway.'

Black eyes bored into her. 'I don't know where your sister is.' Then he turned away dismissively. 'I'm sorry, I can't help you.'

Leah didn't believe him. He was simply being obstructive, a characteristic of his that was not unfamiliar.

She stepped into the hallway right behind him, casting, as she did so, a quick appraising glance round the tiny interior of the flat. So, this was the place that Jo and Carlo had rented for the summer. In spite of its modest size, it looked clean and comfortable.

Vincenzo was striding in the direction of the sitting-room. Leah followed and paused in the doorway to glare at him.

'Why won't you help me?' She narrowed her blue eyes at him. 'All I want is to find Jo and take her home.'

'Then do so.' He had his back to her, as with some impatience he riffled through a pile of books and papers on a desk. 'But preferably do so without bothering me.'

He was silhouetted against the half-shuttered window, a tall powerful figure in a mid-blue suit, his hair against the pure white collar of his shirt as black and as glossy as burnished jet.

Yes, Leah thought without emotion, daring to scrutinise him for a moment, he was undoubtedly a most strikingly handsome man. He always had been and, with the passage of time, those powerful good looks that, once, could take her breath away, had simply matured and grown more refined. He was thirty-three now and in his prime.

Her eyes drifted down to his searching fingers. Long, strong fingers, dark from the sun. Then she snatched away her gaze as a strange feeling tore through her—once she had adored what those fingers could do to her—and in a hard voice demanded, 'What are you looking for? And what

right have you to go rummaging through other
people's things?'

When he pointedly ignored her, she stepped
towards him. 'I asked you a question. What right
have you to go rummaging through my sister's pos-
sessions? And how come you have a key to the
apartment, anyway? Do my sister and Carlo know
that you're here?'

Still, he did not answer her. He pulled open a
drawer and began to search impatiently through the
contents.

'What are you up to? Kindly explain yourself!'
In her irritation she had taken another step towards
him. 'I demand to know what it is you're doing
here!'

He swung round then, slamming the drawer shut,
making Leah jump back at the ferocity of his reaction. Black eyes pierced through her. 'So, you
demand, do you?' His voice was rough metal drawn
against granite. 'I think you are forgetting, *sposa
mia,* that the days when you had a right to demand
anything from me ended a very long time ago.'

He held her eyes as she blanched a little and repeated the words that had caused her to grow pale.
'*Sposa mia.* Had you forgotten? Surely even five
years cannot have wiped from your memory the
fact that you are still my wife?'

'I am not your wife!' His words were like a body
blow, catapulting her back into another time,
another place. But somehow Leah managed to keep
hold of her composure. 'I ceased to be your wife
five years ago.'

'I think not, *sposa mia.*' He had reached out to
seize hold of her. 'Legally, you are still very much

my wife. To my knowledge the marriage has not yet been dissolved.'

'That isn't my fault! I wanted a divorce! You were the one who refused to co-operate!'

'Perhaps it didn't suit me to co-operate, *sposa mia*. But you could have tried again, if you'd really wanted one.' Still holding her, he smiled strangely. 'Is that why you've come to Rome? To try to resurrect our moribund marriage?'

'You have to be crazy!' Leah struggled to free herself. 'The best move I ever made in my life was the day I walked out on you and our marriage. The last thing I'm ever likely to want is to resurrect it!'

'Are you absolutely sure?' He pulled her closer and his eyes drove into her like red-hot skewers. 'Are you absolutely certain that it is not your intention to attempt some kind of marital reconciliation?'

As he spoke, he lightly caught her jaw with his free hand. 'How beautiful you are. More beautiful than ever.' His eyes swept her face and the silky fall of hair. 'A reconciliation, after all, might prove quite enjoyable.'

He was holding her so close that his body burned against her, igniting long-forgotten sensations against her nerve-ends. And it was like a torture to be held there. Leah squeezed her eyes closed. 'Let me go!' she demanded.

In response he let his gaze drift down to her breasts, firm and taut against the cotton of her dress. 'You've filled out a little.' He smiled approvingly. 'You are more of a woman, less of a child.'

Leah could feel anger battling with the anguish inside her. And anger was winning. She pulled herself free. 'Lay a hand on me again and I'll hit you!' she warned him. Her blue eyes flashed. 'I mean it! I'm not joking!'

Vincenzo simply smiled. 'What's the matter? Haven't you missed me? Five years, after all, is a very long time.'

Leah regarded him scoffingly. 'No, I haven't missed you. And five years, I promise you, isn't nearly long enough.'

'In five years, no doubt, more than your body has matured.' He raised one dark eyebrow, the smile still hovering. 'I suspect that by now you are a consummate lover. A reconciliation might indeed prove extremely pleasurable.'

Then his smile grew suddenly as cold as winter. His mouth became a hard and unforgiving line. 'Tell me, *sposa mia,* my faithless little wife, how many men have you had in the past five years? Or are they, by now, too numerous to count?'

Leah felt herself reel beneath the insult. 'How dare you?' she protested. 'How dare you say that?'

He laughed, a hard sound. 'How dare I?' he mimicked. 'I know you, remember?' His eyes burned through her. 'And I know also that the leopardess does not change her spots.'

Leah glanced away. There was nothing she could say. She could not change now what had happened five years ago.

'So, if a reconciliation is what you're after, *sposa mia,* you are wasting your time. I told you at the time that a faithless wife would never again share my life or my bed. And on that, I can promise you, I will never change my mind.'

'Believe me, I wouldn't want you to.' Leah looked him in the eye. 'The only thing I want from you is for you to tell me where my sister is.'

'I've told you I don't know. Your sister is with Carlo. And where that might be is of no great interest to me. I just hope that Carlo is wiser than I was and has the sense not to fall for your sister's little tricks.'

As he spoke, he had turned away to resume his search, rummaging among a pile of newspapers on the coffee-table. Leah watched him with resentment burning through her. 'If Carlo is anything like you, it's *his* little tricks that *Jo* has to beware of. And that's why I'm here. To try to save her.'

'Such sisterly concern. What are you so worried about? Surely your sister's old enough to look after herself?'

'She thinks she is.' Leah grimaced to herself. At the same age—nineteen—she had believed the same of herself. And just look what she'd done! She'd gone and married Vincenzo! And lived to regret it every day of her life since.

She stared at his back, savouring her dislike of him, reminding herself of how he had once almost destroyed her. Jo, she sensed, was bound on a similar road with Carlo. She would not stand by and just let it happen.

'*Eccolà!*'

Vincenzo had found what he was looking for. He pulled out a file from among the pile of papers, flicked it open and swiftly glanced through it. Then

he turned to Leah. 'This is what I came for—a
report that my poor love-smitten nephew was supposed to hand into the office yesterday morning.
Evidently, he had other things on his mind.'

'So, at least he's not entirely like you. That's a
relief.' Leah's tone was cutting. 'One thing nobody
could ever accuse you of was letting your private
life interfere with your work. You always had your
priorities very carefully worked out. Your precious
cars first and foremost and everything else a very
poor second.'

'Carlo's young. He has time to learn.' Vincenzo
met her gaze with a cynical smile. 'Once he's gained
a little experience and had time to realise just how
shallow and meaningless most romantic diversions
in the end prove to be—a lesson which, no doubt,
your sister will teach him—I'm sure he'll soon figure
out what's really important in life.'

'And if he doesn't, I'm sure you'll be only too
glad to tell him. After all,' she added, smiling sar-
castically, 'you wouldn't want anybody working for
Petruzzi Automobili who was less than totally
dedicated to the company.'

'Indeed I would not.' His eyes were unblinking.
'As you just said yourself, the cars come first.'

For some reason, as he said it, Leah's eyes
dropped to his mouth and the hairline scar that dis-
sected his upper lip. And instantly she felt her
stomach tighten and a familiar rush of fear and
anxiety wash through her. She pushed the feelings
from her. They had no place in her heart now. They
belonged to the days when she had loved him,
adored him, before she had come to know he was
not worthy of her love.

Still, she found herself asking him, 'I suppose, these days, your activities are confined more or less to the boardroom? No doubt you've outgrown your passion for the test track?'

He smiled ambiguously. 'How very touching. I had not expected that, after so long, you would still show such wifely concern for my safety.'

'Concern for your safety? Please don't flatter yourself! I promise you, as far as I'm concerned, you're free to climb into one of your precious machines and smash yourself to smithereens any time you like!'

'How very generous of you.' Vincenzo smiled thinly. 'But smashing myself to smithereens, I'm afraid, is not on my agenda. I fear I may end up disappointing you.'

Leah laughed harshly. 'That was something you were always good at.' Then she checked herself abruptly. She was letting him get to her. Pushing back her hair, she turned away, feigning sudden interest in a book on the table behind her.

'Are you going to tell me where Jo and Carlo are?' She tossed the question at him over her shoulder. 'Surely it wouldn't hurt you to do me this small favour?'

'It would hurt a great deal to do you any small favour.' He tossed the observation at her like a poisoned dart. 'But, luckily, that is not a problem. As I've already told you, I don't know where they are.'

Leah shot him a glance. Perhaps he wasn't lying. 'But you could find out where they are. You could talk to your sister.'

'If I was interested in doing so, no doubt I could. But mothers don't always know what their sons are up to.'

At least he was honest about that, Leah thought with a wry smile. His poor widowed mother had at times been driven mad wondering what her wild impetuous son was up to!

She pushed the thought away and turned to look at him. 'But she might know. Will you have a word with her?'

The black eyes looked right through her. 'No, I don't think so.' Then he held up the file in his hand and informed her, 'This is what I came for, and I have work to do now. If you're planning to stay on here, you'd better have this.' He took a key from his jacket pocket and tossed it across to her. 'Hand it in to the porter on your way out. And don't be too long,' he advised her, turning to leave. 'I promised I'd only keep it for half an hour.'

So, now she knew how he'd got into the flat! And she ought to have guessed how right away. Had she forgotten how conniving and ruthless he could be?

She threw him a look of disapproval. 'How much did it cost you to bribe the porter?'

He smiled without remorse. 'The going rate.' Then he paused for a moment in the doorway. 'I trust you won't be staying long in Rome? That is, I *hope* you won't be staying long.' He smiled a lethal smile. 'You would not be welcome.'

'By whom? By you? That won't greatly worry me.' Leah returned a smile that was equally lethal. 'But I don't think my plans are really any of your business.'

'Then allow me to correct you. Unfortunately they are. You are still my wife. You still carry my name. And the name of Petruzzi is respected in Rome. It would distress me greatly if my tramp of a wife were to dishonour that name more than she has already done by getting up to her old tricks again.'

His mouth was a thin line, his eyes like black granite. 'I warn you, *sposa mia*, go back to England. I do not want you here. Do you understand me?'

The unexpected insult had taken Leah's breath away. Her face pale, she glared back at him. 'Oh, how I hate you!' It was suddenly all she could think of to say.

Vincenzo smiled callously. 'The feeling is mutual. So, be warned, *sposa mia*, I am not joking when I tell you that I expect you to leave Rome immediately—and that it would be in your best interests to oblige me.'

He paused for a moment to let his gaze drive through her, his eyes as dark with malice as the eyes of Satan. Then, without another word, he turned and left the room.

CHAPTER TWO

AFTER Vincenzo had gone, Leah sat down at the little desk and scribbled a couple of notes to her sister, giving her the name and number of her hotel and begging her to get in touch immediately.

One she stuck prominently to the fridge door in the kitchen and the other she left downstairs with the porter when she stopped by on her way out to hand in the key. Now she had two more chances of making contact with Jo. She just prayed that her sister would return to the flat soon.

But, as she stepped out of the building and headed back to the Via del Corso, it was no longer worry about her sister's welfare that creased her brow and made her fists clench. What filled her with blind fury were thoughts of Vincenzo.

How dared he insult her and threaten her that way? Who the devil did he think he was? If she wanted to stay in Rome, she would stay in Rome! He was wrong if he thought he could scare her away!

Buoyant with defiance, she turned off the main road and turned into the elegant Via Frattina. Did he expect her meekly to pack her bags and leave with her tail between her legs, just because her presence here didn't suit him? He had a grave disappointment coming if he did!

Anger had made her thirsty. On a sudden impulse she made her way to one of the pavement cafés and seated herself at an empty table. Once upon a time she had been afraid to stand up to him. Flight had seemed an easier option than fighting him.

But not any more. She was no longer a child. She would stay here in Rome for just as long as she needed to. Or, at least, she corrected herself, for her three weeks' holiday—three weeks in which she had been planning to redecorate her flat before all this business with Jo blew up!

She ordered a coffee and a toasted sandwich and sat back to watch the promenade of shoppers. But her mind was still buzzing with thoughts of Vincenzo and those unforgivable insults he had hurled at her. In particular that gibe about dishonouring his name.

It had occurred to her to inform him that she no longer used his name. Back home in England for the past five years, both socially and professionally she had been known as Leah Blain. One of the first things she had done on her return had been to reassume her maiden name.

But she had never got around to changing the name on her passport, so that here in Rome, to her chagrin, she did indeed go under the name of Petruzzi.

As the waiter brought her coffee, she took a quick mouthful. What had he called her? 'My tramp of a wife'? Once again she felt her stomach heave inside her. What had happened had happened, but she was no tramp.

She took a deep breath. But none of that mattered. All the anger and the bitterness between herself and Vincenzo were best forgotten. Water under the bridge.

She laid down her cup and marshalled her thoughts abruptly. It was Jo, her sister, that she must worry about now.

Two days later, in spite of endless phone calls and daily visits to the flat, Leah had still not made contact with her sister. And then, that evening, as she took dinner in her room, suddenly the bedside phone began to ring.

She leapt excitedly across the room to answer it. 'Jo, is that you?' she breathed, grabbing the receiver.

'It's me. I'm downstairs. I want a word with you.'

Leah's heart sank. It wasn't Jo, it was Vincenzo. She was tempted to hang up. 'Well, I don't want a word with you.'

But he cut across her protestations. 'I'm coming up.' Then the phone went dead.

Leah swore beneath her breath. This was really a bit much! Who did he think he was, barging in on her like this?

She glanced quickly at her reflection in the mirror and ran her fingers hurriedly through her hair. Should she quickly change? she wondered, frowning. After all, she was dressed in nothing but a robe. But she shook her head firmly. She wouldn't have time—and, besides, she was damned if she would put herself out for him. And if she had her way, he wouldn't get past the door!

It seemed like only a moment later that she heard the sound of footsteps coming along the corridor.

Mentally, she braced herself for what was coming. A visit from Vincenzo could only mean trouble.

She deliberately took her time about answering his knock. Let him wait, she thought stubbornly, glaring at the door. Then with a deep breath, she crossed the room reluctantly to open the door no more than a crack.

He was dressed in a white suit with a white shirt and a pale tie. She looked into his face. Satan in disguise. 'This visit isn't convenient,' she told him crisply. 'I'm afraid it really isn't convenient at all.'

He glanced down at her attire with eyes like black razors. 'What's the matter? Are you entertaining a lover? I thought I warned you about indulging in such pursuits while you happen to be staying in Rome?'

Leah felt like slapping him. Her hand tightened around the door handle. 'I'm not entertaining anyone, if it's any of your business! I happened to be having dinner!'

'We've already established that it is my business.' His eyes slashed into her. 'Or had you forgotten?'

Leah glared back at him. 'We established nothing of the sort. So kindly just tell me what you want— and then leave! My dinner's getting cold.'

'Are you sure you don't mean your lover's getting cold?' Vincenzo smiled at her cynically. 'Surely that's more your line.'

'Damn you and your endless insinuations!' Overcome by outrage, Leah snatched the door wide and stood aside to let him enter. 'Go ahead! Search the room! Produce this lover I'm supposedly hiding!'

He walked into the room, his stride unhurried, and sat down in one of the chairs without even glancing round. She had been tricked, Leah realised, closing the door behind him. He had known all along that she was alone.

'So, finish your dinner.' He waved a hand at the table where her half-eaten chicken *cacciatora* was sitting. 'Don't let me interrupt you. We can talk while you're eating.'

Just the thought of having to talk to him had taken away her appetite. Leah stood where she was, arms folded across her chest. 'How did you know where to find me?' she demanded.

He smiled. 'That was easy. A couple of phone calls. When it comes to investigations of that nature, the name Petruzzi carries a certain amount of weight.'

Leah grimaced. Quite so. Then she demanded impatiently, 'So, now that you've found me, what do you want? Have you come to renew your demand that I get out of town?'

'And if I have?'

'You're wasting your time. I'll leave Rome when I'm good and ready.'

He smiled at that. 'We'll see,' he told her. With one hand he smoothed the immaculate crease of his trousers as he hooked one leg at the ankle over the opposite knee. He sat back in his seat, hands laid lightly on his thighs. 'But that is not the reason I'm here.'

'Then tell me what is.' Leah glared at him, hating him for the way he was keeping her in suspense.

He unbuttoned his jacket, watching her narrowly. 'First tell me this. Have you made contact with your sister, or has she been in touch with you?'

Leah shook her head. 'No on both counts.' Then she narrowed her eyes at him. 'Why do you ask?'

'There has been a development.' His black brows drew together. 'But perhaps this is something you are already aware of?'

'I'm aware of nothing.'

'Are you absolutely sure of that?'

'Absolutely.'

'I don't think I believe you.'

He was driving her mad. Leah took a step towards him. 'I'm telling you the truth,' she informed him in an even tone. 'So, kindly, for once just take my word for it and get on and tell me what this development is you mentioned!'

Vincenzo responded by leaning back in his chair and eyeing her with infuriating dark-eyed amusement. 'You've changed,' he remarked. 'Where are all the tears and tantrums that I remember from the old days when you didn't get your way?'

A momentary cold flicker of remembrance touched her heart. Deep inside her something squeezed sickly. Yes, she had changed. She had grown wiser and stronger. It would take more than Vincenzo now to reduce her to tears.

Leah looked him in the eye. 'I've grown up,' she told him. 'I've come a very long way since I turned my back on you.' She smiled a thin smile. 'So, take my word for it, you won't find it quite so easy to manipulate me these days.'

He smiled in response, a boldly amused smile. 'Is that a challenge, *sposa mia*? As you know, a challenge is something I rather enjoy.'

'Not a challenge, just a warning.' But she found it hard to hold his gaze. Just for an instant, something in the way he had looked at her had stirred another, more sexual sort of memory. Just for a heartbeat she had glimpsed the fire in him, the excitement, the passion that had once consumed her soul.

Protectively, she folded her arms across her chest. 'Well,' she demanded, 'are you going to tell me about this development?'

'Of course I am. That's what I'm here for.' He had glimpsed, she sensed, that momentary reaction. He had always been good at reading behind her eyes.

But the moment had passed. She regarded him coolly. 'But you're not going to tell me just yet, are you? First, you want to play your little power game, keeping me in suspense, making me wait a while.' She narrowed her eyes at him. '*You* haven't changed.'

In response, he simply shrugged. 'I was fine as I was.' Then the humour left his eyes as he leaned towards her. 'Tell me the real reason you've come to Rome.'

Leah sighed elaborately. 'I've already told you—but OK, we'll play it your way, if you insist. I have no desire to spin this encounter out unnecessarily.'

With composure she seated herself in the chair opposite him, adjusting the front of her robe as she did so.

He noted the action. 'Such virginal modesty. You are forgetting, *sposa mia,* that I am your husband. I know very well what lies beneath that robe. And, should I have forgotten and wish to refresh my memory, all I would need to do is reach across and disrobe you.'

Leah felt herself flush. A foolish reaction. But his words had sent a strange sexual flutter through her. 'You are not my husband.' Her voice was unsteady. 'And if you try to lay a hand on me, I'll scream the place down.'

'Yes, you always were extremely responsive.' He smiled a strange smile, making her blush deepen. Then his smile vanished abruptly. 'Perhaps that was the problem. One man simply wasn't enough for you.'

It was hard not to respond, not to leap to her own defence, but somehow Leah forced herself to remain silent. She dropped her eyes momentarily, then raised them to meet his again. 'I was about to tell you why I've come here—although I warn you it's the same story I told you before.' She hurried on before he could change the subject. 'I came here to persuade Jo to come back to England before she makes a terrible mistake with Carlo.'

As he watched her unblinkingly, dark eyes cynical, she decided to elaborate a little. 'You see, I had a letter from her a couple of weeks ago saying that she was planning to stay on here after the summer. And she can't do that. She's due to start university. She can't throw away her future for some worthless boy.'

'As you did.' He was not slow to pick up her allusion. 'I seem to remember your situation was similar. When we met you were planning to start a course at art college.'

She was surprised that he remembered. Coolly, she assured him, 'Indeed I was. I only wish I'd known then what you yourself pointed out the other day—that in life one's career is far more important than any meaningless romantic diversion. I learned that lesson late. But better late than never.'

'You took up your art studies?'

'Yes, and I completed them.'

'Congratulations.' He smiled a mocking smile. 'It must have been reassuring for you to discover that you were actually good at something.'

'Meaning?' She glared at him.

'Meaning, *sposa mia,* that as a wife, as we both know, you were a consummate failure.'

'And you, I suppose, as a husband, were a raging success?' She held his eyes and laughed a scoffing laugh. 'I've never in my life met anyone less suited to marriage!'

'Only because I chose the wrong wife.' His tone was steely, his dark eyes cruel. 'I should never have married someone who was clearly not up to the task.'

You should never have married someone you didn't love! The protest tore through her, but she could not say it. Even now it hurt to admit that cruel truth.

But he was continuing, 'So, after college, what did you do? Don't tell me you went out and found yourself a job?'

'And why should that surprise you?' His tone had offended her. 'Why would I not go out and get a job?'

Vincenzo smiled and shook his head. 'I'm afraid you never struck me as the independent type. Quite the opposite, as a matter of fact. You always seemed a little lost when there wasn't someone around to look after you.'

Leah felt herself wince. Had she really been like that? 'No doubt that was because I married too young.' Her tone was calm, slightly cutting. She forced herself to let his cruel dig wash over her. Once, as he knew, she would have risen to it in anger, but these days she'd learned to control her emotions.

'My mistake was,' she continued calmly, 'that I went straight from my parents' care into yours. I never had a chance to stand on my own two feet.' With a smile of satisfaction she crossed her knees, carefully adjusting the hem of her robe. 'But all that has changed, I'm happy to say. For the past couple of years I've been working as a fabric designer for a very well-known company in London.'

As she named the name, Vincenzo nodded. 'Very impressive,' he observed sincerely. 'It would appear, then, that the year you wasted with me did not have such a devastating effect on your life.' His tone was scathing. 'I'm pleased to hear it.'

Leah smiled back at him, though it was not easy. 'The year I wasted with you,' she informed him evenly, 'had no effect on me whatsoever. As far as I'm concerned, it's as though it never happened.'

She stared at him fixedly, praying he couldn't guess that what she had just uttered was the biggest lie of her life. That wasted year, as she had blithely called it, was burned in her heart and in her memory for ever. To recall the pain of it and all the pain that had followed, even now, could leave her breathless and shaken.

Not that he cared. He simply smiled at her. 'What a coincidence. I feel exactly the same.'

She had always known that. She smiled at him cynically. 'So, you see, I would prefer to spare my sister the inconvenience of such an empty and time-wasting experience. I don't want her to make the same mistake that I made.'

'Then you know more than you're telling me?' Suddenly, he had leaned forward. 'You already know that they are planning to marry?'

Leah blinked at him. *'Marry?'* she gasped in horror. 'Who said they were planning to marry?'

'You didn't know?'

'Of course I didn't! I had no idea things had got that serious!'

Vincenzo sat back and regarded her narrowly. 'You're quite sure this isn't part of some plan you've cooked up to pay back me and my family for some imaginary slight?'

Some imaginary slight! Leah almost felt like laughing. She still bore the scars of the wounds he had inflicted, wounds that had been very far from imaginary!

But that was not the issue now. Jo's welfare was what concerned her. And suddenly she felt angered by his callous cynicism. She straightened in her seat. 'Are you seriously suggesting that I'd consider for one moment using my sister to get back at you? In what way is she supposed to pay you back? By marrying Carlo and making his life a misery? Isn't that rather a twisted idea? Even for you?' she put to him crudely.

He raised one dark eyebrow and laid his hands on the chair arms, his long fingers dark against the creamy-pale silk. 'Perhaps,' he conceded. 'But that isn't what I was suggesting. What I was suggesting was that your sister's marriage to Carlo would bring you back into closer contact with me. That might suit you very well if by some chance you were still planning to stick a knife in my back.'

He smiled with dark amusement and held her eyes. 'I seem to remember your once making such a threat—and, who's to tell, perhaps you still intend to carry it out?'

Had she really made so violent a threat? Leah's stomach curled. She knew it was likely. After all, she had said so many wild things, striking out blindly like some tormented animal. But at the time it was herself she'd been trying to destroy. Anything to put an end to the pain.

But not any more. She had conquered the pain. And she no longer felt any need for revenge. It was enough that the past was finally behind her.

Or would have been but for this hiccup with her sister—although, as she looked into his face, full of careless dark arrogance, she felt moved to inform him with a malicious little smile, 'Don't worry, I have no plans to stick a knife in your back. I assure you, if I were ever to go to such homicidal lengths, I would insist on the pleasure of looking you in the eye as I stuck the knife in.'

She paused, allowing her smile to curl with pleasure at the corners. 'I wouldn't stab you in the back, I'd stab you straight through the heart.'

Vincenzo watched her carefully from beneath long black lashes. 'Yes, I believe you would,' he observed with a dry smile. Then he raised his eyes and ran one hand across his hair. 'So, it's safe to take your word that you're not in any way involved in this?' He raised an interrogative eyebrow. 'Is that the case?'

'I keep telling you it's the case.' Leah breathed impatiently. 'Why do you have such trouble believing what I tell you?'

'Perhaps because you have such trouble telling the truth.'

'And where do you get that from?' Leah laughed a caustic laugh. 'As I recall, *you're* the one with that particular failing!' Her heart twisted as she said it and her eyes grew cold with rancour. He had almost destroyed her with his lies.

But there was no remorse in the eyes that looked back at her, only an icy rancour equal to her own. 'And *you're* the one who has trouble keeping her vows. Perhaps that's why I have such difficulty trusting you.'

Their eyes locked for a moment, like those of two gladiators in combat. One could almost hear the clash of cold steel. Then, abruptly, dismissively, Vincenzo rose to his feet and strode across the room to stand with his back to her.

'It's really neither here nor there whether you knew about the marriage or not. The only thing that matters is that it must be stopped. As long as Carlo was simply having a bit of fun, that was really of no interest to me...'

He half turned round and flung her a glance over his shoulder. 'But I will not allow another member of your family to further pollute the name of

Petruzzi! I will not allow this marriage to take place!'

The insult stung like a slap in the face. Leah caught her breath and sharply informed him, 'I'm in complete agreement that the marriage must be stopped...but it's my sister who's in danger of being polluted. I'd die before I'd allow her to become a Petruzzi!'

Vincenzo dismissed her with a sweep of his lashes. 'Don't worry, *sposa mia,* it will never happen. That is something I have already promised my sister.'

So, he had, after all, spoken to his sister. Leah herself had tried to call her that very morning, only to discover that she had moved house. 'Was it she who told you they were planning to get married?'

'No, I heard that story from a friend of Carlo's. My sister was horrified when I told her. Unfortunately my brother-in-law is in the States at the moment, so he's not in a position to do anything about it. But I am.' He smiled grimly. 'And I fully intend to. This is one marriage that will never take place.'

He meant it. She could see that. And he would stop at nothing. When Vincenzo made up his mind on some course of action there was no force on earth with the power to divert him.

But his methods could be crude. Heavy-handed. He didn't care if he trampled all in his path. And Leah knew her sister. She could be as obstinate as a mule, especially when others tried to lay down the law.

Leah rose to her feet now and took a deep breath, stuffing her hands in her pockets as she stepped forward to face him. 'I shall help you to stop the marriage,' she told him in a cool tone. 'This is something, in my opinion, that we ought to do together.'

'Is that so?' He looked back at her candidly. 'In that case, I'm afraid, our opinions differ.'

'I have good reason for believing it would be the wise thing to do.' Leah continued as though he had not spoken. 'My sister can be difficult, but she'll listen to me. I'm one of the few people who knows how to handle her.'

'Don't worry, I'll handle her. I don't need your assistance. And when it's all over I'll deliver your sister back to you.'

In small, broken pieces, Leah thought with a small shudder. She took another step towards him. 'I'm afraid I can't agree to your handling this alone.' She looked him in the eye and grimaced. 'I know how insensitive you can be and I don't want my sister hurt any more than is necessary.'

Vincenzo smiled at that. 'Me? Insensitive? I wonder where you got that idea?'

'Yes, I wonder.' Leah's tone was sarcastic. Then she took a deep breath and narrowed her eyes at him. 'That's why I intend to play a part in whatever happens. Consider me a human shield, if you like.'

He smiled again, his dark eyes cynical. 'What a noble proposal, and how uncharacteristic.' Then he shook his head. 'But I'm afraid not, *sposa mia*. I intend to handle this on my own. All you would do is complicate the situation.'

'I wouldn't! I'd make it easier!'

'I don't think so.'

'Jo would listen to me!'

'She'll listen to me.'

'She won't! I know her!' Leah bit back her rising anger, knowing that if they were to fight she could well lose the battle. She took another step towards him and smiled persuasively. 'Believe me, our task will be much simpler if we do whatever needs to be done together.'

Unexpectedly, his eyes softened. 'Is that so, *sposa mia*?' His gaze roamed her face. 'Is that what you believe?' All at once one hand was on her waist. 'Tell me more about this unexpected co-operation you're proposing.'

She had been wrong to soften her stance against him. She might have known he would only take advantage. With a gasp of impatience Leah stepped abruptly back.

It was the sharpness of the movement that caused his hand to catch momentarily in the belt of her robe. And as the belt loosened, the front of the robe fell open, causing Leah to grab hurriedly in an effort to close it. But Vincenzo was too quick for her. She felt her stomach tighten as his fingers reached out to take hold of the soft fabric.

'Just a moment.' He held her eyes deliberately, and suddenly she was remembering his earlier remark about how easy it would be to reach out and disrobe her.

Her heart jumped inside her. She started to pull away, but with firm fingers he was holding her a prisoner in his grasp. Then suddenly he smiled. 'Don't worry, *sposa mia*. As I told you, my memory is very good. I really have no need to refresh it.'

Then, with firm supple movements, he pulled the robe closed and unhurriedly tightened the belt at her waist.

'There. You can relax now.' He smiled at her knowingly. 'And let's just forget all this talk of co-operation. Co-operation was something we were never very good at.'

Leah could not speak. For some reason she was trembling. She was still trembling long after he'd turned and left the room.

CHAPTER THREE

LATER that evening, as she was climbing into bed, the bedside telephone rang again.

Automatically, Leah reached out for the receiver, then she froze for an instant, her stomach twisting strangely. Could it be Vincenzo? What could he want of her? The thought of talking to him suddenly made her feel uneasy.

Then, as the phone rang again, she took a deep breath and snatched the receiver quickly to her ear.

'Leah, it's me. I got your message. I'm sorry I missed you at the apartment.'

'Oh, Jo, it's so good to hear you!' Relief went rushing through her at the sound of her sister's voice. 'Where are you?' she enquired. 'Are you back in Rome?'

There was a momentary pause. 'No. We're at the seaside. I phoned to see if there were any messages, and Mario, the porter, read me your note.' Another short pause. 'Why have you come here, Leah?'

'You know why I've come here. I told you in my letter.' In spite of her concern, Leah kept her tone light. The last thing she wanted was to antagonise her sister. That would be a certain recipe for disaster.

Jo let out a sigh. 'Look, I know what I'm doing. And I've made up my mind. Don't try to stop me.'

'I just want to talk to you. Tell me where you are.' Leah felt herself tense as she asked the next question. 'You haven't done anything foolish, have you? You haven't gone and married Carlo?'

'And what would be foolish about that?' Jo shot back at her. 'I happen to be in love with Carlo. Why shouldn't I marry him, if that's what I want?'

Leah held her breath. 'But you haven't, have you?'

'No, not yet.' There was a note of resentment. 'Not that it's really any of your business.'

'Of course it's my business! I'm your sister and I love you!' With an effort Leah checked her rising impatience. 'Look, please just tell me where you are. I just want to talk to you, that's all.'

'There's nothing to talk about.' Jo was stubborn. Then her voice changed suddenly. 'Look, I can't talk now. Carlo's just come in.' She giggled delightedly. 'I think he's brought me a present—some beautiful seashells from the island.' There was another muffled giggle, then she told Leah, 'Please just go back to England and don't think of interfering. I'm very happy and there's nothing to worry about.'

An instant later the phone went dead. Leah banged down the receiver in dismay and frustration. Nothing to worry about? You're crazy, little sister! She clenched her fists. If only you knew!

With a helpless sigh, she sank back against the pillows. It looked as though Jo was dead set on her own ruin and there was nothing that Leah could do to stop her. She thought of Vincenzo and had a sudden vision of him barging in on the lovers like a bull in a china shop. With Jo in her current stubborn frame of mind, his rough tactics, she felt doubly certain now, would simply have the opposite effect. Assuming, of course, that he managed to track them down!

In that instant a thought like a thunderbolt struck her. She sat up abruptly. Suddenly she had the solution! She knew how she could persuade him to include her in his mission!

And there wasn't a moment to lose. She must act immediately. She snatched up the phone and punched in a number, marvelling at the way she remembered it so easily. Then she held her breath as the number began to ring.

At last a voice answered. *'Casa Petruzzi.'* Petruzzi residence. It was the voice of the housekeeper.

Leah took a deep breath. *'Signor Vincenzo, per favore.'* Then, before the woman could ask, she added briskly, *'Qui parla sua moglie.'* This is his wife.

There was a delay that seemed to last for an eternity. Then a gruff voice spoke. 'Yes. What do you want?'

'I've got to talk to you. I'm coming over.' Before he could protest, she slammed the phone down.

Just for once, she was calling the shots!

It was a fifteen-minute ride by taxi to the fashionable residential quarter of Parioli, and it was well after midnight when, with a crunch of tyres, the cab turned in through the gates of the Villa Petruzzi.

Just as she remembered, the rosy-red façade, with its balconies and elaborately shuttered windows, was lit up by a battery of discreetly placed floodlights. Nothing had changed. It was all as grand as ever. Suddenly Leah's heart was beating like a drum.

The big front door at the top of the double stone staircase opened as she climbed out and paid the taxi driver. Biting back her nerves, she hurried towards the front door, expecting to see Grazia, the housekeeper, waiting for her.

But it wasn't Grazia. Instead, standing in the doorway, was a tall dark figure in white trousers and black shirt.

'Isn't this a little late for a social visit?' Vincenzo scowled at her, not even feigning a welcome.

'What's the matter, isn't it convenient?' Leah looked him in the eye without a flicker of repentance. He wasn't the only one who could descend on people without an invitation. 'But this isn't a social visit,' she assured him. 'I have a little deal I want to discuss with you.'

'Then I'm afraid it will have to wait until tomorrow.' He continued to stand like a rock in the doorway, apparently with no intention of inviting her in. 'I don't usually discuss deals at this hour of the night.'

'So, you've changed your ways?' Her tone was harsh with irony. 'I thought business matters regularly occupied you at this hour?' At least, that was the story she'd once been expected to believe—though, of course, she'd known otherwise, as night after night she'd lain alone and chafing in their big double bed.

But his past infidelities were not worth dwelling on now. She cast these thoughts from her and looked him straight in the eye. 'However, I think you ought to make an exception this time. The deal I want to discuss concerns Carlo and my sister.'

He straightened fractionally. 'You've heard from your sister? Have you found out where they are?'

Leah smiled enigmatically. 'I may have done— but I don't intend discussing it here on the doorstep.' Pointedly, she paused, knowing she had hooked him. 'However, if you're not interested...' she pretended to turn away '...perhaps you'd do me the favour of calling me another taxi.'

'You'd better come in.' He was stepping aside, opening the door wide so that she could pass into the hall.

'Are you absolutely sure?' She feigned unwillingness. 'I would hate to inconvenience you if it's really too late for you.'

But she had had her invitation and he wasn't offering another one. 'Come in if you're coming and go if you're going.' His tone was sharp. 'I'm in no mood for games.'

Leah dallied not a moment longer. Quickly she stepped past him and into the huge hall—and, instantly, it was as though an avalanche had hit her. The paintings on the wall, the scattered Persian rugs, the imposing curved staircase leading to the upper floors. Once this magnificent place had been her home. An ache throbbed within her. And how she had adored it.

'Come this way.'

As Vincenzo strode past her, she reminded herself swiftly of a more relevant truth. She might have adored it in the beginning, but she had soon grown to hate it, just as she had grown to hate the man with whom she had shared it. The day she had escaped had been the best day of her life.

He was leading her into one of the sumptuous reception rooms and inviting her to take a seat. Not daring to look around her lest all the memories swamp her, Leah perched uneasily on the edge of one of the velvet armchairs, her eyes on Vincenzo as he crossed to the bar.

'What will you have?' he enquired over his shoulder.

'Nothing. An orange juice.'

'A bit mild for you? Have you lost your taste for the hard stuff?'

Leah felt herself stiffen. She knew what he was referring to. She wasn't likely to forget that shameful episode in her life. She threw him a hard look. 'I don't need it now. Not since I got you out of my life.'

He merely smiled as he poured himself a Scotch and emptied a can of orange juice into a glass filled with ice. He crossed the room unhurriedly and came to stand before her.

'Congratulations.' His tone was mocking. 'It's nice to know you've mended your ways.' He held out her drink to her, his eyes piercing through her. 'But then, as we both know, there was much room for improvement.'

'Indeed there was.' Leah looked back at him coolly. 'Five years ago I had neither wit nor judgement—a fact that was borne out by my marriage to you.'

As he responded with a wry smile, more amused than insulted, and crossed to seat himself in the sofa directly opposite her, Leah cradled her drink and eyed him beneath her lashes.

In spite of the passionate tenor of his nature, she had learned that it took a lot to rile Vincenzo. Insults and harsh words, for the most part, slid off him. And that duality in him had always intrigued her. The apparent contradiction was part of his attraction.

She smothered the thought quickly. It was simply part of his deviousness! And no one in their right mind could find deviousness attractive!

And it was then, as she cast a more malicious eye over him, that she suddenly fancied she could detect in his dress a faint lack of his usual immaculate perfection.

From the way his shirt was tucked into his trousers one might suppose that he had dressed in a hurry. And the black hair had a faintly rumpled look to it, as though he had combed it carelessly, with his fingers.

Perhaps she really had caught him at an inconvenient moment. Perhaps he had been entertaining one of his girlfriends.

She arched an eyebrow at him and let her gaze slide over him as she took a mouthful of her orange juice. 'I really am sorry if I interrupted you. If you were otherwise occupied, I do apologise.'

He knew what she was getting at. 'Don't worry about it.' He smiled across at her and confided, 'I never have any trouble in picking up where I left off. But then, that is something you already know.'

As he held her gaze, Leah snatched her eyes away, ashamed of the warm glow that had spread through her innards. She took a gulp of her orange juice, as though to douse it. 'Do I? I'm afraid I've forgotten,' she lied.

'No doubt you have.' His expression never altered, though a cold note had crept into his voice. 'With all the lovers you must have been through by now, remembering who was who must pose something of a problem.'

Leah caught her breath inwardly. These insults were deeply wounding. 'I suppose you've been living like a monk?' she countered crisply.

'Not exactly.' His dark eyes were shuttered. Then he shrugged impatiently. 'But none of this matters. We're both free agents—or at least we soon will be.'

Leah arched one eyebrow. 'What exactly does that mean? Do you mean you're finally going ahead with the divorce?'

But Vincenzo was not about to be sidetracked. Impatiently, he swirled the whisky in his glass. 'You said you'd come with news about Carlo and your sister.' His tone was sharp. 'Let's just stick to the subject.'

Leah looked back at him, unblinking. 'Very well,' she conceded. Her tone was neutral. The possibility of divorce—or any other aspect of their relationship—was not a subject she had any desire to get embroiled in. She sat back against the cushions, laid her glass on the side-table and carefully crossed her legs in their narrow blue trousers. 'I didn't say I'd come with news about them. What I said was that I'd come to talk about a deal.'

'I thought you said you knew where they were?'

'I didn't say that. I said I might know.'

'Then you've heard from your sister?'

'I had a phone call.'

'And?' His tone was growing impatient. 'What is it going to require for you to tell me what you know? Do I have to draw it out of you with pincers?'

'No, I'm going to tell you. That's what I'm here for.' As she paraphrased his words of a couple of nights ago, she smiled a smug smile. The tables were turned now. 'But before I do, I require your promise...'

'What promise?'

'Your promise that you won't go alone to confront them. You have to agree to take me with you.'

'That's out of the question!' He laid his glass down and leaned towards her, his eyes hard and implacable. 'I intend to deal with this situation my way. I don't need any help from you.' He thrust his chin at her. 'I thought I'd made that plain?'

Leah stood her ground. 'And I thought *I'd* made it plain that I intend to come with you? Besides, you're in no position to do it alone. I know you think you're God Almighty, but allow me to remind you of one small detail—you don't even know where Jo and Carlo are! By the time you track them down they could already be married. We can't afford to waste any time.'

The black eyes glinted. 'Then tell me where they are.'

But Leah shook her head. 'Only if you promise.'

'I'm not promising anything. I've already told you that. So kindly just tell me where they are!'

Wasn't this just typical? He was totally unreasonable! Overcome with frustration, Leah jumped to her feet. 'Damn you!' she exploded.

'Why must you be so difficult? Surely what I'm asking isn't so much?'

Black eyes bored into her, then suddenly he put to her, 'If you know where they are, what do you need me for? Why don't you just go off and confront them on your own? Why come here, trying to make deals?' His eyes narrowed dismissively. 'You're lying, *sposa mia*.'

'No, I'm not lying!' Leah glared down at him. 'I didn't say I knew *exactly* where they are, but I have a couple of clues, which is more than you have!'

'So, what are these clues?'

'I don't intend telling you! Not until you've agreed to my demand!'

He said nothing for a moment, just looked up at her in silence. Then with a weary sigh he rose to his feet. 'OK, you win. I'll do as you want. I'll take you along if you'll tell me what you know.'

Leah could scarcely believe it. 'Promise?' she demanded.

He nodded and smiled. 'I promise,' he responded. Then, his eyes still on her, he reached out one hand and flicked a tendril of hair across her shoulder.

Leah felt herself shudder as his hand brushed her cheek. She wanted to step away, but she forced herself not to. Such a reaction would appear ridiculously childish—and yet she felt uneasy standing so close.

She looked up into his face and her stomach tightened. That soft look in his eyes was a look she had forgotten. Infinitely seductive, infinitely sensuous. Once she would have died to feel him look at her like that.

Her breath caught in her throat. 'Well?' he was asking. 'Aren't you going to tell me your secret?'

Her eyes drifted to his mouth and the scar on his lip. Foolishly, she longed to reach out and touch it. That scar, so long ago, had caused her so much heartache.

Leah took a deep breath and fought hard to concentrate. 'They're staying at the seaside. I don't know whereabouts. But there's an island. Jo said Carlo had been there, collecting seashells.'

She saw his lips move. 'Is that it?' Then he smiled as she nodded and his hand touched her cheek as he pushed back another loose tendril of hair. 'That wasn't hard, was it? We didn't need to fight. You should have told me right away.'

'Does it mean anything to you? Do you know where it is?' Leah swallowed hard and raised her eyes to his. 'Will it help us to track them down?'

'I think it might.' Vincenzo nodded. 'I have a suspicion I know where that island might be.'

'Then we must go tomorrow. Straight away. Is it far? How long will it take us?'

Vincenzo smiled, but his eyes had grown cold. 'It won't take me long. A couple of hours. But, I'm sorry to disappoint you, you won't be coming along.'

'What do you mean?' It was as though he had struck her. In an instant she was jolted back to her senses. 'You can't go back on your word! You promised!'

'Did I?' He stepped away from her and picked up his drink. 'So, what's one more broken promise between us? There have been so many already. One more won't matter.'

Leah felt herself swallowed on a wave of anger. He really meant it! Deliberately, he had tricked her!

'You can't do this! I won't let you get away with it!' She clenched her fists and glared across at him. 'I'm coming with you! You can't stop me!'

Vincenzo shook his head. 'Sorry, *cara*. I think you'll discover that I can.' He drained his glass and glanced at his watch. 'It's getting late. I'll order a taxi for you.' Then he smiled at her callously. 'I'd like to get to bed, so I can make an early start tomorrow morning.'

'You unscrupulous bastard! How can you do this? Doesn't a promise mean anything to you?'

By way of an answer he ignored her totally and crossed to the phone that lay on a side-table. He picked it up and punched in some numbers, then spoke into it in rapid Italian.

He laid the phone down again and turned arrogantly to face her. 'Your taxi will be here in about ten minutes.' He smiled and gestured at her unfinished orange juice. 'While you're waiting, you may as well finish your drink.'

Leah would gladly have thrown the glass of orange in his face, but she resisted the temptation and turned away furiously. There was no point in begging or trying to plead with him. That was something she had learned a long time ago. He was immune to female tears. He was callous to the marrow. And, besides, she would die a thousand deaths before she would go down on her knees to him.

They passed the next ten minutes in total silence, then, right on time, the doorbell rang.

Vincenzo strode past her. 'Let's go,' he commanded. And, without bothering to look at her, he headed out into the hall.

Leah trudged behind him, stiff with fury. He was totally immoral, totally without conscience. How could she have been so foolish as to trust him?

As she stepped into the hall, he had already reached the front door and was pulling it open, inviting her to leave. Then he was reaching into his trouser pocket and withdrawing a wad of bank notes. 'This should be more than enough to cover your fare,' he was saying.

But halfway across the hall, Leah suddenly hesitated. Why should she just obey him, like a lamb to the slaughter? She had to think of Jo, of what was best for her, and she couldn't leave her sister's fate in his hands.

On a sudden defiant impulse she turned on her heel and went racing back into the room she had just left, slammed the door shut and turned the key in the lock.

'I'm not going!' she shouted. 'I'm spending the night here! And then I'm going with you in the morning!'

She heard him swear in Italian as he strode back across the hall. Then the door-handle rattled. 'Come out of there this instant!'

'I won't come out until you repledge your promise!'

He cursed again. 'Then you can stay there all night!'

'OK, I'll stay! That's all right with me! And I'm coming with you tomorrow whether you like it or not!'

She could feel the violence of his anger pulsing through the door, as though he might wrench the door from its hinges to get at her. But the next moment, to her relief, she heard him recross the hall and disappear outside—to pay off the taxi, she imagined. Then a minute later he was stepping inside again and the front door closed with a bang behind him.

Leah held her breath. What would happen now? Would he come and try to force her to open up the door?

But he did no such thing. It was as though he had forgotten her. She heard him climb the stairs, then the hall light switched off and suddenly she was quite alone in the room, the only sounds to keep her company the ticking of the French clock on the mantelpiece and the frantic beating of her own heart.

CHAPTER FOUR

LEAH scarcely slept a wink that night.

The sofa where she curled up was perfectly comfortable, as comfortable as any bed. But sleep wouldn't come. There were too many ghosts here. They seemed to prod at her like relentless fingers and awaken all the memories that were locked in her head.

Staring into the night, she found herself remembering the very first time she had arrived at the villa, wide-eyed with happiness, with her new husband at her side.

'It's so beautiful!' she'd gasped. 'I never dreamed it could be so beautiful! Vincenzo, you never told me you lived in a palace!'

He had laughed and kissed her. 'A palace for a princess. Only the very best is good enough for my bride.'

Ah, yes, in those days he had known how to woo her, turning her heart to putty with soft words. And how she had adored him. Totally. With a full heart. No heart had ever loved more completely than hers.

To be truthful, she had loved him from the first moment she had met him that day in her father's little office. It was her father who had introduced them. 'Signor Petruzzi, meet my daughter. Leah, this gentleman has come all the way from Italy to make an offer for poor old bankrupt Blain Cars.'

'Poor, perhaps, but a name worthy of respect.' A cool firm hand had reached out to clasp hers. 'I'm very pleased to meet you, Miss Blain.' Then, with a glance at her father, he had added in a sincere tone, 'I hope you're aware, in spite of your father's modesty, that this company of his has a worldwide reputation?'

Leah had been touched by this spontaneous kindness. Her father's little company, once his pride and joy, had been on the slide for several years now, ever since the major heart attack that had nearly crippled him, and his self-esteem had taken a serious battering.

She had smiled with gratitude at the handsome young Italian. 'Yes, I know,' she had answered. 'I'm very proud of him. And I'm as sorry as he is that he's having to sell up.'

Vincenzo had nodded sympathetically and turned his dark eyes back to her father. 'I'm here to offer your company a good home, Mr Blain. As part of Petruzzi Automobili I can promise it will be given a new lease of life.'

It was one of the best offers her father had had. Petruzzi Automobili, manufacturers of prestige cars—easily in the same league as Ferrari and Lamborghini—was one of the top car manufacturers in Europe. Which was why Leah had been somewhat taken by surprise to discover that their company chairman was a young man of twenty-seven. Though even then Vincenzo had exuded a sense of power that left one in no doubt as to his competence.

And he had evidently wanted Blain Cars rather badly. Over the weeks that followed he was in constant contact with Leah's father's little company in the heart of Surrey. 'It's that new gearbox we recently developed that he's particularly interested in,' her father had explained to her. 'He reckons it can be adapted for use in his own cars.'

But that, apparently, was not the only thing Signor Petruzzi was interested in. To her astonishment and delight, on his second visit to Surrey he invited Leah out to dinner.

That evening she had had her very first taste of what it was like to be treated like a princess. It was a magical evening. Unforgettable. That evening her heart had been lost for ever.

'Do you know, you have the bluest eyes I have ever seen?' Vincenzo had leaned across the restaurant table towards her. 'When I look into those eyes I see liquid sapphires. A man could drown in eyes like these.'

Leah had blushed and gazed back at him, her own heart drowning. His sophistication, his confidence was something totally new to her. She was used to the company of awkward young boys— nineteen-year-olds, the same age as herself.

Vincenzo had poured them more wine and pushed her glass across to her. 'There is only one place in the world that can match the blue of your eyes, and that is the Mediterranean on a bright summer's day.' He took a sip of his wine. 'Have you seen the Mediterranean? Have you ever visited my part of the world?'

She had shaken her head. 'I've been to the Adriatic and a couple of times to the south of France, but I've never been to the south of Italy...'

'Then you haven't seen one of the true wonders of the world.' He had smiled that smile that could turn her limbs to water. 'One day, if you will allow me, I will show it to you. There are so many things I would love to show you.'

That was when Leah had started to dream. And he had fuelled her dreams and given them wings. Regularly he came to Surrey to wine and dine her, flying over from Rome just for the weekend. And during the week he would phone her endlessly, sometimes two or three times a day.

'I love you,' he had told her. *'Ti amo, cara mia.'*

And, her heart awash with happiness, she had answered, 'I love you, too.'

They had become engaged just two months later, and a month after that, in a breathless rush, they were married in her local church in Surrey. In the meantime, the deal with her father had been signed and Blain Cars had been taken over by Petruzzi Automobili.

'He made me an offer I couldn't refuse,' Leah's father had joked when he broke the news. 'And I couldn't be happier with the way things have turned out. This way, everything stays in the family!'

And, as it turned out, he had made the deal just in time. Just a few months later, tragically, he was to die, the victim of a second heart attack.

But at least he had had the pleasure of seeing his elder daughter happily married to the man she loved—for in those days no one could have been happier than Leah. Each day seemed to her like a dream come true and with each day she was a little more in love with her husband.

They had spent their honeymoon on the Petruzzi yacht, lazily sailing the blue Mediterranean. And it was there that she grew from a girl into a woman. It was there she learned the secrets of marital love.

Leah came to her husband an innocent virgin. Excited, eager, just a little anxious. And he had taken her and tutored her with gentleness and patience, teaching her the delights and pleasures of her own body, lovingly instructing her in the mysteries of his.

The first time they had made love would live with her for ever. She had not known human flesh was capable of so much pleasure.

She had gasped at his kisses and moaned beneath his caresses, her senses in flames, her loins aching with the wanting of him.

'Please!' she had beseeched him, her fingers tangling in his hair. 'I want you, Vincenzo! Please don't make me wait!'

But he had simply continued to caress and torment her till every nerve-end glowed with exquisite anguish and every muscle in her body throbbed with longing. Her hands reached for him shamelessly, urging him to join her.

Then at last his own hunger could wait no longer. As he mounted her, he kissed her. *'Sposa mia cara!'* Then with one fluid movement he had entered her, and tears of sheer joy had risen to her eyes.

'I love you! I love you!' he had whispered. 'Always I will love you. Always, my love!'

Leah sat up with a start now and looked around her, for a moment confused, uncertain where she

was. She could feel her heart thundering inside her
and her cheeks were damp with newly shed tears.

She brushed them away. She must have dropped
off—and what crazy, dangerous dreams she'd been
having! To remember such moments was only to
invite bitterness, for she knew now how meaningless they'd really been.

In spite of what he'd told her, Vincenzo had never
loved her. She'd learned that just a few weeks after
her honeymoon. And she'd learned it right here, in
his very room.

With a sigh of impatience she swung her legs
down from the sofa. Why was she torturing herself
with these memories? She had never forgiven him
for his cynical deception, but she had long ago
driven it from her mind. And it was by forgetting
that she had managed to survive.

Sunlight was squeezing through the closed
wooden shutters, dappling the room with early
morning light. Leah peered at the French clock on
the mantelpiece. It was just before seven. Time she
was up and about.

She ran her fingers through her hair as she
crossed to the window, pushed the shutters open
and drank in the morning air. There were no sounds
of life in the house or in the garden and it seemed
likely that Vincenzo hadn't yet left. Though it was
possible, she knew, that he had slipped out without
her hearing. He was perfectly capable of such a
mean feat.

But it was just at that moment that she heard the
sound of voices, coming, she thought, from the
back of the house. It was time she made herself
presentable and tried to find out where he was.

I'll use the downstairs bathroom, she thought to herself, heading for the door that led out into the hall. She turned the key and pulled the door open. Then she stopped in her tracks, catching her breath, as she nearly went walking straight into Vincenzo dressed in a knee-length towelling robe.

'So, you haven't left yet? I was rather hoping you might have. And from the looks of you you passed a rather disturbed night.'

He smiled as he said it, evidently pleased that she had suffered, his eyes surveying with open amusement her tousled hair and rumpled shirt and trousers. 'You should have asked for a loan of some pyjamas. It's never very satisfactory sleeping in one's clothes.'

You possess pyjamas? She very nearly said it. In the old days he didn't have a pair to his name. He hadn't needed them. He always slept nude.

He seemed to read her mind. 'I keep a couple of pairs for emergencies. You would have been most welcome if you'd asked.'

He certainly wasn't wearing any pyjamas at the moment. Beneath the blue towelling robe, she could sense instinctively, he literally wasn't wearing a stitch.

The realisation sent a treacherous warm glow through her. Annoyed at herself, she took a step back.

His hands were in his pockets as he surveyed her calmly, quite clearly not at all stirred by *her* nearness! 'Are you leaving now, or will you be having breakfast first?'

'I'm leaving when you are. Had you forgotten? You and I are going to find Jo and Carlo.'

'Correction. *I* am going to find the lovebirds. You, if you are wise, will be going to book your flight home.' He smiled a caustic smile, his gaze flickering over her. Then, before she could answer, he turned on his heel. 'I'm going to have breakfast now,' he informed her over his shoulder. 'Suit yourself whether you join me or not.'

Leah watched him go. Oh, I'll be joining you, she informed him silently. Until you leave this house, I won't be letting you out of my sight!

Ten minutes later, washed and brushed, and feeling just a little less dishevelled, Leah joined him at the big circular table in the bright sunny breakfast-room at the back of the house.

He glanced up from his newspaper. 'Just help yourself. There are rolls and croissants, and some eggs on the sideboard. And I'm sure if there's anything special you fancy Grazia will be only too happy to oblige you.'

'I don't want anything special. Just coffee and a croissant.' Suddenly she felt awkward, like an unwelcome guest, in this house that, once, had been her home.

But it was never really my home, she thought with sudden bitterness. I never really belonged here. He never really wanted me.

Leah swallowed back the flood of resentment that suddenly threatened to overwhelm her. These feelings were inappropriate. They belonged to the past. And it was years since she had felt even a trace of such bitterness. This house was doing crazy things to her.

She reached for the jug of orange juice and poured herself a glassful. 'What time are we leaving?' she enquired in a calm voice.

His eyes lifted from his newspaper. 'I'll be leaving when I'm ready.' Then, deliberately, he smiled into her eyes. 'Note my use of the first person singular. As I keep telling you, you are not included in my plans.'

He deeply enjoyed thwarting her. She could see that in his eyes. Leah held his gaze. 'Well, I'm coming with you, whether I'm included in your plans or not.'

Vincenzo shrugged. 'We'll see,' he told her. Then he sat back a little in his chair, surveying her. 'Why didn't you sleep in one of the spare rooms? It couldn't have been too comfortable spending the night on that sofa.'

'It was comfortable enough.'

'Nevertheless, I don't normally expect my house guests to rough it. You'll be giving the Villa Petruzzi a bad name.'

'I thought I'd already done that?' She snapped her response at him. For some reason it had irked her to be referred to as a house guest. Then, she added in a clipped tone, 'Please don't worry about me.' Not that she supposed for one minute that he had. 'I'm sorry if your concern for me caused you to lose sleep.'

Vincenzo smiled at that. 'No need to be sorry. As a matter of fact, I slept rather well.'

'And did you manage to pick up where you left off?' She held his eyes, piqued by his composure, and made a deliberate reference to what he had said last night. Though she doubted now that there had been some woman keeping his bed warm—unless she had left very early or was still asleep.

He took a mouthful of his coffee. 'Alas, I slept alone.'

'A rare occurrence.'

'If you say so.' He paused for a moment and let his eyes drift over her. 'And how about your own sleeping arrangements these days? Do you have someone to share your bed?'

The answer was no. No one shared her bed. The only man who figured at all in her life was merely a friend, not a lover. But she resented the casual way Vincenzo has asked the question, somehow implying that her morals were equally casual.

She eyed him with annoyance and told him bluntly, 'I don't really think that's any of your business.'

'Don't you? I thought it was.' He lifted one eyebrow. 'I thought husbands had a right to know that sort of thing.'

Leah took a deep breath. 'You're not my husband. Not in any real sense of the word.'

'I suppose that's true.' He reached for a brioche, broke it in two and spread butter and honey. 'It is rather a long time, *cara sposa mia,* since you and I were husband and wife in any real sense.'

There was something about the way he said it that caused a ripple inside her. Quite involuntarily, her eyes drifted to his chest, darkly tanned, sprinkled with fine hairs and generously visible in the open V of his robe. And her breath seemed to catch deep within her for a moment, as she remembered in a sudden torrent of sensation the warmth and the virile power of that torso, how wonderful it had felt to be pressed against it, to feel the beat of his heart, the raw excitement of his flesh. It was indeed a long time since she had experienced such pleasure.

She dragged her gaze away abruptly, faintly shocked and furious with herself. 'As I already told you...' she took a mouthful of her orange juice '...I stopped thinking of you as my husband a long time ago. At home I don't even use your name any more. These days I'm known as Leah Blain.'

His gaze never flickered. 'That is undoubtedly a good thing. To carry the name Petruzzi demands adherence to certain standards.'

Leah let that pass. Let him think what he wanted. It was sufficient for her self-esteem that she herself knew the truth about the standards she adhered to.

She straightened in her chair. 'While we're on the subject, perhaps you wouldn't mind answering a question? Why did you oppose me three years ago when I tried to get a divorce?'

She'd always wondered about that. According to English law, after a separation of two years a divorce could be granted if neither party objected. Yet, when her solicitor had written to Vincenzo's, requesting his co-operation in the matter, he'd received a curt reply in the negative.

'Considering how much you hate having to be associated with me,' Leah put to him, 'I would have thought you'd have been all too eager to see the back of me.'

'I'd already seen the back of you—or so I thought.' A barbed smile flitted across his face. 'And, besides, I was not in the mood to be co-operative. Perhaps it would have suited you to be free at that time? Perhaps you were planning to remarry? I saw no reason to oil your adulterous wheels for you.'

Yes, that figured. 'I see. Sheer bloody-mindedness. I might have guessed that was what was behind it.' Leah refrained from adding that she'd had no plans to remarry, that she found it hard to envisage herself ever doing so—one bitter experience was more than enough!—and that her only motivation had been finally to be free of him. Let him wonder! It was none of his damned business!

'However, things have changed.' He smiled obliquely. 'Three years ago it made no difference to me whether we were legally divorced or not. It was enough for me that you had returned to England.' He sat back in his seat, his dark eyes narrowed. 'Now, as I say, the situation has altered.'

'You mean you want the divorce?'

He nodded. 'As soon as possible. I had intended writing to you, via my solicitor, on the matter. Your unexpected visit has saved me the trouble.'

He smiled a thin smile as he warned her, 'And forget about playing tit for tat. Now that we've been apart for more than five years there's nothing you can do to prevent the divorce going through.'

Leah was aware of that. 'Don't worry,' she assured him. 'I'm as eager as you are to have this mockery of a marriage ended. It's already gone on far too long, as it is.'

'So, for once, we are in agreement?'

'It would seem so.'

'Then all that remains is for us to decide which one of us should start proceedings. I suggest you leave that honour to me. That is, if you have no objections?'

'None whatsoever.' But she was mildly curious. 'So, what's brought on this most welcome decision? I hope you're not planning to remarry,' she told him. 'To have made one woman's life a misery is surely enough, even for a sadist like you?'

Vincenzo looked back at her and shook his head slowly. 'It was you who made your own life a misery. You wanted more than I could give.'

'I know.'

I wanted love, she thought with a twist of sadness. You gave me passion. You gave me excitement. You opened up a whole new wonderful world to me. And I would have died for you, for those glorious black eyes of yours, for the curve of your mouth that, even now, if I'm honest, can touch my heart with longing and regret. But what I craved most you couldn't give me. You couldn't give me a simple thing called love.

Suddenly, her heart was beating painfully. She dropped her eyes to the blue and white tablecloth. All at once she had almost felt nineteen again. Desperate, vulnerable, longing to go to him. Longing to feel his arms about her—warm, strong arms that could make her forget anything in way she had experienced in the embrace of no man since.

No, it had not all been bad. It would have been easier if it had.

'Will you be arranging your own transport back to the hotel? If you have a word with Grazia, she'll call a taxi.'

His words wrenched her rudely back to the present. Leah glanced up abruptly, her thoughts still swimming, and answered him with amazing coherence.

'I'm not going back to the hotel. I'm going with you, so don't try to tell me that I'm not. You made a promise and I won't let you back out of it.'

'And how do you plan to stop me?' He was watching her over his newspaper. 'Tell me. I'd be most interested to know.'

Leah pursed her lips. 'I'll find a way.'

Vincenzo laughed a mocking laugh. 'That should be interesting.' Then with a shuttered look he shot her a challenge. 'How do you even know that I'm planning to go and look for them? Maybe I have better things to do today.'

She hadn't thought of that. 'And do you?' she demanded.

'Perhaps. Perhaps not.' He was being deliberately infuriating. 'I can't really see that it's any of your business.'

Leah clenched her fists. She felt like hitting him. 'Are you or are you not planning to go and find them?' she demanded. 'I want an answer! I want to know what's happening.'

'And what difference can it possibly make to you? As I've already told you, you're not coming.'

'Damn you! Just tell me!'

'Finish your breakfast.' His eyes lanced right through her. 'And kindly stop badgering me. I'd like to finish my own breakfast in peace.'

'All I'm doing is asking a civil question!'

'And I have just given you a very civil answer!'

'You haven't given me any damned answer at all! Why can't you just answer questions with a simple yes or no? Would it hurt you to be straightforward for once in your life?'

Vincenzo threw down his newspaper. 'And would it hurt you to stop going on at me like the Spanish Inquisition? I'm not answerable to you! You seem to be forgetting. I don't have to discuss anything with you that I don't wish to!'

'You really are incredible!' Leah laughed a harsh laugh. 'You think everything has to be done your way, according to your rules, the way it suits you! Don't you ever stop and think of others just occasionally? Doesn't it ever occur to you that your way might be wrong?'

She snatched a quick breath, her bosom heaving. 'You're the most unreasonable, self-centred man I've ever in my life had the misfortune to know! You think the world revolves around Vincenzo Petruzzi, that the rest of us are just there to do your bidding! Well, that doesn't apply to me any more! I won't just let you trample over me! I won't stand for it! Do you hear me? Not any more!'

As she stopped herself short, the silence was deafening. Shame flooded through her. She felt her cheeks flame. Just for a moment she'd been transported to the past and all the quarrels that, towards the end, had been such a vivid part of their life together.

The victim of some brainstorm, she had suddenly felt, as real as though they were still a part of her, all the hurt and the anger that had assailed her five years ago. And it had all come pouring out of her. She could not have stopped it.

She clenched her fists in her lap and dared not look at Vincenzo. 'I'm sorry,' she said. 'That was quite out of place.'

It was a relief when at that very moment the phone across the room began to ring. Leah was aware of Vincenzo rising to his feet and crossing without a word to answer it.

He picked up the receiver. *'Pronto?'* she heard him say.

Leah gathered herself quickly, breathing deeply. What on earth had come over her? How could that have happened? She poured herself some coffee and spooned in some sugar, then lifted the cup with a still shaky hand and forced herself to take a sip. Whatever had triggered it, one thing was for certain, it must never be allowed to happen again.

Vincenzo was signing off. *'Ciao, Franca,'* he was saying. *'Parleremo fra poco.'* We'll speak again soon.

Then he was laying down the receiver and crossing back to Leah. She heard his footsteps, though she did not glance up at him.

As he paused by the table, her heart was still thundering. Perhaps, she was thinking, she should just get up and leave. It would save her the indignity of being thrown out.

She could feel his eyes on her, piercing right through her. She opened her mouth to speak, staring at the carpet. 'I think I ought to go now,' she heard herself saying. 'I can't really see any point in my staying.'

There was a momentary pause. She sensed him glancing at his watch. 'I'll be leaving in fifteen minutes,' he advised her. 'If you want a lift, kindly be ready.'

CHAPTER FIVE

LEAH was waiting resignedly in the hall when
Vincenzo at last came down the stairs, dressed in
white trousers and a deep blue shirt and carrying
a bulging tan leather weekend bag. It looked, after
all, as though he was definitely planning to go in
search of Jo and Carlo.

She rose to her feet, her eyes flickering to his
face. What's happening? her eyes asked him. Are
you taking me with you or dropping me off at the
hotel?

But she resisted the urge to put these questions
into words. He had already made clear how he felt
about her questions and there had been more than
enough upset for one day. Whatever his plans, she
would know soon enough. It would be pointless,
anyway, to try to persuade him further.

'Are you ready?'

She nodded.

'Did you have time to have some breakfast?'

'I had some coffee and a croissant.' For some
reason, she was finding it difficult to speak. Her
jaw felt stiff, her throat dry and hoarse. All she
longed for was to be gone from this house.

He nodded and led the way briskly across the
hall. Then a moment later, out in the bright sunshine, she was following him down the stone steps
to the waiting car.

'*Prego.*' With cool politeness he held the passenger door open for her before depositing his bag in the boot of the car.

Leah settled herself in the leather bucket seat and stared with unseeing eyes, fixedly, through the windscreen. A large part of her was resigned to the fact that he would dump her back at the hotel. And it would probably be for the best, she decided. This excursion to save her sister was rapidly turning into something else—a kind of sordid re-examination of her long-defunct relationship with Vincenzo.

It was unsettling and it was unhealthy and it was doing her no good, and the sooner she put a stop to it the better. The only trouble was Jo. How on earth would she find her? She gritted her teeth. I'll do it somehow.

Her hotel was in the city centre, a stone's throw from the Spanish Steps. And that was where they were headed, it quickly became obvious. All her efforts to persuade him had come to nothing.

They drove slowly through the crowded traffic, exchanging not a word, Leah never once glancing in Vincenzo's direction.

I don't need to, she thought miserably. I can feel his presence all around me, wrapping me in its power, squeezing me dry. And, as hard as she tried to concentrate on the scenes all around her—the throngs of tourists, the buildings so full of history— in her mind's eye the only image she could see was the dark-eyed face of the man seated beside her.

I shall be grateful for some time on my own, she decided. Time to chase these demons from my head.

Then suddenly they were drawing up outside the entrance of the hotel. Still, without glancing at him,

Leah reached for the door handle. She was halfway out of the door when he spoke.

'How long will it take?' The question was brusque.

Leah paused to frown at him. 'How long will what take?'

He held her gaze for a moment, his expression unreadable. 'How long will it take you to pack a bag? You'll need a few things if you're coming with me.'

Leah blinked. Was she hearing things?

'You haven't changed your mind, have you?' He smiled up at her thinly. 'You do still want to come, I take it?'

So, she hadn't been hearing things! She nodded her head vigorously. 'Ten minutes. It'll take me ten minutes,' she assured him.

Then she turned and flew excitedly through the hotel's main door.

Less than twenty minutes later they were on their way, following the signs for the *autostrada* south. Leah buckled firmly into her seat, wondering what had caused Vincenzo to change his mind, yet not daring to ask in case he changed it again.

Instead, as they headed towards the approach road of the motorway, she enquired, 'Where exactly are we going?'

'A place called Paluro, down in Campania. I've a pretty strong feeling that's where they might be.'

'What makes you think that? Is there an island there? Have you been to Paluro before?'

Vincenzo cast her an amused glance. 'So many questions.' He held her eyes for one brief, revealing instant, then turned his attention back to the road. 'However, this time, just to keep the peace, I'll do my best to answer them for you.'

It was a clear and pointed reference to her earlier little outburst. Leah felt a brief warmth touch her cheeks. It would appear her accusations had simply amused him. He was enjoying reminding her what a fool she had made of herself.

'The answer to your final question is no, I haven't ever been there, though I know the surrounding area quite well. But Rosella and Giuseppe—my sister and her husband, Carlo's parents,' he elaborated unnecessarily, 'they have a summer villa in Paluro, and I'm sure I've heard them talking about some nearby island where they go and have picnics and gather shells and things.'

'Are they staying there now?'

'No, the house is empty. Giuseppe's on business in the States,' he reminded her, 'and Rosella is spending the summer in Rome. It would be a perfect place for Carlo to take your sister. I think there's a pretty good chance we'll find them there.'

Leah felt her spirits lift. 'It does sound likely.' She crossed her fingers mentally. 'I hope you're right.'

'Well, we'll see soon enough.'

They were on the *autostrada* now, filtering into the fast lane, the big car speeding effortlessly, like a bird. Leah cast a sideways glance at Vincenzo, at the assured hands on the wheel, and felt a flutter of excitement in the pit of her stomach.

In the old days she'd used to tell him he drove like a demon, but the real truth was that he drove like an angel. To be seated beside him, as with consummate skill he coaxed and controlled the powerful engine, handling the sleek automobile with an almost passionate mastery, was an experience to make the blood sing in your veins.

But then the ability to make the blood sing in her veins was one that Vincenzo had always possessed in abundance. It was the passion he injected into everything he did, whether it was driving or making love—or quarrelling!

The memory, unexpectedly, brought a smile to her lips. At times, it had been like living with a volcano, but their life together had never been boring. On the contrary, it had been a daily emotional adventure. He had known a thousand different ways in which to inspire and excite her.

She felt a dull sensation dampen her spirits. It had been so long since she had experienced such excitement, such an exhilarating sense of the simple joy of living. Certainly, no other man had ever made her feel it. Though she had never really been aware of the lack, until now.

'So, what are we going to talk about for the next couple of hours? It'll take us at least till lunchtime to get to Paluro.' Cutting through her thoughts, Vincenzo posed the question. 'Or would you rather just listen to some music?'

'I don't really care.' She did not look at him. If she listened to music, her thoughts would wander, and that might not be a very good thing. Her thoughts had developed an alarming propensity to stray into areas that had long been forbidden. But at the same time the prospect of a cosy little chat didn't really hold much appeal.

'Tell me about yourself, what you've been doing. You must have been doing something over the past five years.'

'I expect I have.' His flippancy irked her. A good part of that five years, if only he knew it, she'd spent healing the scars that he had inflicted. But her tone was neutral as she went on to tell him, 'I spent three years studying design at art college and the last two working for that company I mentioned.'

'You enjoyed your time at college?'

'Very much. I made lots of friends and I adored my studies.' Then she surprised herself by adding proudly, 'I graduated second in my class.'

'Congratulations.'

She wasn't sure if he was mocking her, but what did it matter if he was? She knew how much she'd achieved during her years at college and also over the couple of years since she'd left. And her achievements had not been purely professional, though professionally she'd achieved more than she'd ever dreamed.

But she'd also made strides in other directions. For one thing, she'd grown up, she'd learned to stand on her own feet and—perhaps the most vital achievement of all—she had finally, painfully, come to realise that the world did not start and end with Vincenzo.

'And do you live in London? I know your work's there.'

'I have my own flat.' Again, there was pride in her voice. And she had a right to be proud, she reminded herself firmly. She'd worked damned hard, doing extra weekend and evening jobs, in order to save for the downpayment.

'I would never have believed it.'

At least, *that* was genuine! 'But then you never had very much faith in me,' she countered, feeling a sudden hot flicker of hostility and a corresponding reluctance to confide in him further.

She shifted her gaze away and put to him crisply, 'But why this sudden interest in me? Isn't it just a little out of character? Why don't we talk about you instead? As we both know, that's what really interests you.'

He did not bat an eyelid. 'It's as good a subject as any.' Then he flicked her an amused glance. 'So, what do you want to know?'

Leah felt like saying, 'Nothing', and in one sense it was true. But there was a treacherous corner of her mind that was, in spite of everything, mildly curious. About why, for example, he was suddenly so keen for the divorce. Was he, as she had suggested, planning to remarry?

But there was no way in the world that she intended to ask him outright. It was not so important to her, after all, that she would give him the pleasure of knowing she was interested.

She shrugged elaborately and did not look at him. 'Tell me whatever you want to. It doesn't really matter. We both know how much you enjoy the sound of your own voice. I'm sure you'll manage to think of something.'

'I can think of many things. It's been a busy five years.' His tone was light and mocking, refusing to rise to her sarcasm. 'So, where would you like me to begin, *sposa mia?* With things professional or matters more personal?'

Leah shrugged with what she hoped looked like total indifference. 'Oh, I know all about Petruzzi Automobili and the huge successes it's been having worldwide.'

'Do you indeed? You flatter me, *cara,* that you should continue to take an interest in my company.'

'Please don't be flattered. I take no interest whatsoever. But one can't help reading the occasional newspaper headline.'

'You'll know, then, that Blain Cars is doing well, too. I think your father would have been pleased by its progress.'

His voice dropped as he said it, on a note of respect, and Leah was aware of a resentful tightening in her stomach. Her father had been genuinely fond of Vincenzo and Vincenzo had made a show of feigning fondness in return. But then he was good at faking emotions he didn't feel—at least for as long as it was useful for him to do so.

Still, what he'd just said was true—her father would have been thrilled at the way his ailing company had prospered. But she deliberately refrained now from thanking Vincenzo for the one and only promise to a Blain, one of all the dozens that he'd made, that he'd actually had the decency to keep. Instead, she said,

'Since you went to all the trouble of buying it, I assume it was in your interests to build it up.' She threw him a cool glance. 'Why else would you have bothered?'

'Quite right. Why else?' he conceded, irking her. 'So, you see, like you, I've been working pretty hard. At the car plant we employ three times the previous workforce and sales in the US have more than doubled.'

He smiled. 'But I'm sure none of this really interests you. Perhaps you'd prefer me to tell you something about my private life instead?'

Unaccountably, Leah's stomach tightened. Of course, he was bound to have had a private life that he had pursued with the same passion that he put into his cars. It had been unrealistic to imagine that, like herself, he had virtually substituted work for more personal diversions.

She drew herself up short. Was that really what she had imagined? She must have been crazy. Out of her head. A man of Vincenzo's vigorous sexual appetites was not likely to deprive himself for long of fleshly pleasures.

The thought caused a rush of sensation in her loins. Once it had been she whose pleasure it had been nightly to satisfy those sexual appetites that had aroused equally vigorous appetites in her.

She thrust the thought from her. It was shameful and inappropriate. Without looking at him, she informed him in a cool and distant voice, 'I'm afraid I have no wish to hear about your private life.'

'That's a new development. It always used to interest you. I seem to remember a barrage of questions every time I was out of your sight for more than a few seconds.'

Leah swallowed, her cheeks flaming, hating him with a passion. Though it shamed her, she knew his accusation was true. She really had been that insecure.

She threw him a hard look. 'Isn't it funny how things change? You could have a hundred secret liaisons going on these days and it wouldn't interest me in the slightest.'

'No?'

'Why should it? You mean nothing to me. You're just a bad memory. That's all you've been to me for a very long time.'

'Good. I'm glad to hear it.' He shot her a thin smile. 'Since it looks as though we're destined, over the next couple of days, to spend quite a lot of time in one another's company, I would hate to think that I might have to endure one of your jealous little scenes.'

Damn him for mocking her! Those scenes had been his fault! Considering all his other women, no wonder she'd been jealous!

Leah turned on him, white-faced. 'You know, you're a real bastard! I'd forgotten just how much of a bastard you are!'

'Had you? How remiss of you.' His tone was taunting. 'On the contrary, I have forgotten none of your faults.' Then he smiled suddenly, unexpectedly, and shook his head slowly. 'You know, I think this may not be such a bad idea—you and I going together to find the errant lovers. It's only just struck me this very minute.'

As he paused, Leah turned to him, 'Oh?' she enquired. 'Don't tell me you're admitting that I was right and you were wrong?'

Vincenzo cast her a quick glance, dark eyes steely behind the smile. 'It just struck me that the pair of us offer a pretty compelling argument as to the basic incompatibility of the Petruzzis and the Blains. A quick half-hour in our abrasive company ought to convince them, if anything can, that they're heading for disaster.

'After all,' he added with biting emphasis, 'who in their right mind would want to end up like us?'

Who indeed? He was absolutely right. Yet in a perverse way she felt insulted by the observation.

'Well, at least there's one big difference between them and us,' Leah retaliated, her sharp tone disguising her resentment. 'As far as I can gather, they're in love with one another.'

Vincenzo did not look at her and did not try to deny her hidden accusation. How could he? Leah thought. They both knew he had just used her.

Instead, he said, 'Even if they are, it makes no difference to the outcome. There isn't going to be any marriage.' With an impatient gesture he reached out towards the dashboard and pressed the button on the CD player. 'On the whole, I think music was the better idea.' He turned up the volume. 'Let's just skip the conversation.'

To the strains of Verdi's *Rigoletto* Leah sank back gratefully in her seat. Talking was even more of a minefield than thinking. Every subject they touched on seemed to awaken some new ghost.

She turned to gaze out at the hurrying landscape. Please let Jo and Carlo be at Paluro, she prayed silently. Let me do what must be done, as quickly as possible, and then just let me go back home again.

Back to normality. Out of this man's clutches. Away from all the painful memories he stirs up. As far away from this place as possible. Back to the precious safety of the new life I've built.

*   *   *

'Where are you going? You've gone right past it! There was a sign to Paluro just fifty metres back! Didn't you see it? You should have turned off!'

'Keep calm, *sposa mia*. I know what I'm doing.' Vincenzo reached forward to turn down the volume of the music. 'First, we'll have lunch and then we'll go in search of the lovers. I don't enjoy trauma on an empty stomach.'

'I thought trauma was something you enjoyed at any time.' It was an unnecessary dig, but Leah couldn't resist it. 'Don't tell me you're mellowing in your old age?'

'Isn't that what one's supposed to do in one's old age?' Vincenzo threw her a look of black-eyed amusement. 'You know me. I always go by the rule book.'

Leah laughed in spite of herself. 'That'll be right!' The only rules he ever obeyed were those he made himself!

Then she turned to him and frowned, 'But I think we should go straight there. Every minute could be vital.'

She was wasting her breath. 'We'll go after lunch. It won't take long and, besides, I'm hungry.'

Leah was, too. She decided not to argue. Instead, she asked, 'So, where are you taking me?'

'I'm taking you to where we'll be staying. It's not far. We come off at the next turn-off.' He flicked the indicator and moved to the inside lane. 'We'll be there in less than twenty minutes.'

His mood had noticeably softened over the past hour or so. That terse mocking note had vanished from his voice and his features seemed less harsh,

more relaxed. The Verdi—and the lack of conversation—had evidently done him good.

Leah felt quietly grateful as she sat back in her
seat. If they could manage to keep the atmosphere
between them light, devoid of emotion, free of an-
tagonism, this trip might prove to be just bearable.
She took a deep breath. She would be civil if he
was. After all, she hadn't come here to fight.

Soon they were heading down the magnificent
coast road, the sea like an endless blue mirror to
the right of them, hills dappled with orange-groves
and ochre-coloured buildings stretching on the other
side as far as the horizon.

Then they were taking a right and turning into a
wide driveway that led to a large villa, shaded by
tall palm trees.

Leah turned to Vincenzo, a frown on her face.
'What's this?' she demanded. 'This isn't a hotel.'

'You're right, it isn't. It's a private villa. What's
the matter, don't you like it?'

How could she possibly not like it? It was quite
magnificent, set in sumptuous gardens, a stone's
throw from the sea. No doubt it belonged to friends
of Vincenzo's who'd offered to put them up for the
duration of their stay.

'I'm surprised, that's all. I was expecting a hotel.'
What really surprised her was the fact that Vincenzo
was willing to appear with her in front of his
friends. There was something pleasantly straightforward and open about the gesture. Not his usual
devious way of doing things at all.

As he parked beside the main door in the shade
of some trees, he explained to her, 'Trying to find
a hotel room at this time of year is like looking for

a needle in a haystack. They're all booked up. It's the holiday season.'

Even so, Leah thought to herself, suddenly intrigued by the situation, if she had been asked to lay bets she would have thought it more likely that he would have had them sleep in a field somewhere before he would ever entertain this controversial solution.

And, she had to confess, it was secretly rather reassuring to realise that he was not, after all, as bitterly ashamed of her as she had always supposed.

'Vincenzo! Amore! Eccoti, finalmente!'

A woman was standing in the doorway. Beautiful, dark-haired, wearing a bright, flowing caftan. Then an instant later, she was rushing towards Vincenzo, arms outstretched, her face alight with pleasure.

'Franca! Cara mia!' Vincenzo caught her and hugged her. Then he kissed her and murmured some inaudible endearment.

As though caught up in a dream, Leah watched the little scene, suddenly, from out of nowhere, remembering.

Franca.

Of course. That phone call at the Villa Petruzzi that at the time had barely registered. *'Parlaremo fra poco,'* he'd said. I'll speak to you soon.

But now Vincenzo and the woman were turning towards her. 'Let me introduce you to Leah,' Vincenzo was saying, leading the beautiful Franca by the hand. 'Leah, meet Franca. Franca, this is Leah.'

'So, you're Vincenzo's ex-wife. I'm so pleased to meet you.' Franca extended her right hand in a friendly greeting, but not before Leah had caught the flash of diamonds from the magnificent ring on her other hand.

And suddenly she understood why Vincenzo wanted the divorce and why he had been so reluctant to bring her here in the beginning.

Her suspicions had been right. He *was* planning to remarry. And the beautiful Franca was his future bride.

CHAPTER SIX

'ACTUALLY, I'm his wife, not his ex-wife.' Leah looked the dark-haired woman in the eye as she said it, wondering why she had taken such an instant dislike to her and why the error had irked her so much.

She shot a swift sidelong glance in Vincenzo's direction and smiled with mock politeness before adding, 'I point that out only in the interests of accuracy. I wouldn't like you to be under any misapprehension.'

Franca simply smiled. 'Of course. My error. I assure you it wasn't my intention to jump the gun in any way.'

Oh, no? Leah thought silently with a twist of cynicism. That ring on your finger tells a rather different story!

Then, lest anyone should misinterpret her re-action—heaven forbid that it should be miscon-strued as possessiveness!—she looked around her with a generous smile. 'What an absolutely beauti-ful place you have here!'

'Thank you. I must say I'm rather fond of it myself.' Franca responded with an equally charming smile—though Leah could sense that, behind the charm, a sharp incisive brain was sizing her up. Then, 'Come,' Franca invited, turning to include Vincenzo, 'let's go indoors and I can show you your rooms before we have lunch.'

She paused a fraction, one eyebrow lifting as she let her eyes drift back to Leah. 'Or, in view of what you've just pointed out regarding your marital status, perhaps that should be *room*, not rooms?'

Leah looked her in the eye and smiled without humour. Ten out of ten for poise, she was thinking. And mentally she sharpened her claws.

'No, you were right first time. Definitely *rooms*.' Besides, she added to herself, I wouldn't wish to deprive you of your bedmate for the night.

Throughout the brittle exchange Vincenzo had said nothing, but Leah could sense, almost tangibly, his enjoyment. No doubt the faintly sordid spectacle of his fiancée bickering with his estranged wife appealed to his arrogant sense of humour. He probably deluded himself that they were bickering over him.

Which was definitely not the case, as far as she was concerned, Leah assured him silently with a cool cutting look, as Franca proceeded to lead them indoors. Franca was more than welcome to him, gift-wrapped.

They had lunch out on the terrace, overlooking the sea, and for Leah, at least, it was an uneasy experience.

Franca was a perfect hostess, warm and attentive and utterly charming—and the sort of person, Leah found herself thinking confusedly, whose company, normally, she would rather have enjoyed. As it was, that instant antipathy she had felt remained lodged in her throat, as immovable as a fishbone. And when, over the roast veal, the conversation got round to the impending wedding, the feeling grew so strong that she almost felt she was choking.

'Of course, after the wedding, I'll be moving to Rome and this place will only be used at weekends.' Franca smiled regretfully and slid a teasing glance at Vincenzo. 'I hope you appreciate the sacrifice I'm making for love? I've lived here all my life. I'm really going to miss it.'

Vincenzo smiled back at her and took a mouthful of his wine. 'You'll soon get used to living in Rome. Before very long you won't miss this place a bit.'

'Maybe you're right. And what choice do I have?' Franca shrugged a small shrug and glanced at Leah. 'I can scarcely go on living here after we're married and leave my poor husband all alone in Rome.'

The entire discourse was making the hairs on the back of Leah's neck positively quiver with irritation. She laid down her fork and observed almost curtly, 'Your poor husband could always move in here and commute to Rome, then you wouldn't have to move.'

'Oh, I couldn't dream of asking him to make such a sacrifice. Rome's his home. He's a Roman to his fingertips.' She slid a warm smile in Vincenzo's direction. 'Isn't that so, *caro*?'

Vincenzo nodded. 'Absolutely. And Romans don't transplant easily anywhere else.'

As intransigent as ever, Leah thought to herself. Not even his love for the beautiful Franca could change his selfish, overbearing ways. She hated the way that made her feel better.

But at last the ordeal of lunch was nearly over. As coffee was brought, Vincenzo glanced across at her. 'We ought to be thinking about making a move soon. Maybe we can catch the errant lovers while they're having their siesta.'

'I couldn't agree more. I think we've wasted enough time.' Pointedly, Leah folded her napkin.

But in spite of—or perhaps because of—her impatience, Vincenzo seemed inclined to linger. He insisted on drinking two cups of coffee, then on disappearing upstairs to his room, 'Just to freshen up quickly,' being the excuse he offered.

'I'd better come with you.' Franca leapt to her feet. 'Just to check that you've got plenty of towels and things. You don't mind if we leave you alone for a minute?' she added with a quick, apologetic glance at Leah.

Leah shrugged her consent. 'I'll wait out in the garden.' A likely story! she was thinking to herself, as she pushed back her chair and headed out into the hallway. Freshening up quickly? Checking on towels? More likely the real purpose of this stolen tryst was to indulge in a bit of unbridled physicality. Leah's presence over the past couple of hours, she sensed, had severely inhibited the lovers' ardour.

That was, she thought, as she stepped outside, unless Vincenzo had changed radically over the past five years. When she was engaged to him he couldn't keep her hands off her!

Happy days, she thought with just a twist of bitterness. Who could have guessed at all the heartache that was to follow?

She sat down on one of the cool stone benches and gazed out unseeingly over the sun-dappled flowerbeds. In those days she had believed that their love would last for ever, that nothing and no one could ever come between them. She closed her eyes and smiled wryly to herself. Who in the world would ever have thought that one day, on the brink of divorce, she would end up as a guest in the home of his new fiancée?

At the sound of voices heading towards her, Leah turned round abruptly and felt a sudden rush of anger. There they were, strolling across the garden, arm in arm, heads bent together. It was enough to make you sick, she decided.

As they came closer, Franca raised one hand and waved to her. 'Hi!' she called out. 'I hope you're not bored waiting?'

Leah ignored the question and looked right through her as she rose impatiently to her feet and turned with a scowl to address Vincenzo.

'Are you ready to go? It's getting late.' Her tone was as prickly as a bag full of hedgehogs. Suddenly she was blindingly furious with both of them for putting her in this degrading position.

Did they really think it was fitting and right to parade their sordid little relationship in front of the woman who was still Vincenzo's wife? Did they have no taste at all? No sense of propriety? Didn't the whole thing strike them as just a little tacky?

Vincenzo smiled smoothly, unchastened by her anger. 'Ready when you are,' he responded without a flicker.

'I've been ready for the past fifteen minutes!' The nerve of him! Leah glared at him hotly. 'What did you think I was doing—counting the palm trees? I've been sitting here waiting for you!'

'Well, since I'm here, let's go,' he suggested with just the hint of an irritating smile. Then, still with Franca glued to his side—like a limpet, Leah thought to herself as she followed behind—he was heading down the path to where the car was parked.

'When will you be back?' Franca continued to hover as he pulled open the passenger door to let Leah slide inside.

'I'll ring if we're going to be terribly late.' As he kissed Franca's proffered cheek, Leah cringed and stared ahead. With every second that passed the woman grated more on her nerves. Her stomach was literally boiling inside her.

But at last they were heading off down the driveway, while the figure in the brightly coloured caftan stood in the doorway to wave them off.

Leah cast a quick, disparaging glance at her rapidly receding reflection in the wing-mirror. 'Well, at least she didn't insist on coming with us,' she muttered bad-temperedly to herself.

'Would you have objected if she had?' Vincenzo picked up the remark. She ought to have remembered, he had ears like a cat.

'Of course I would have objected! What's going on with Jo and Carlo is no business of hers. No business at all.'

They were heading for the approach road to the motorway. As Vincenzo manoeuvred his way amongst the traffic, just for a moment he didn't answer. Then he turned towards her briefly, black eyes curious. 'You appear to feel very strongly about it.'

Did she? That halted her. She bit back her emotions. 'I'm simply annoyed at the way she detained you. We should have been on our way to Paluro hours ago.'

If she were to tell him that she was annoyed at the tastelessness of the situation, he might twist that round and read something false into it. He might even have the vanity to suggest that she was jealous. Hadn't he already had the gall to warn her on that score?

He threw her a glance. 'I wouldn't worry about it. Nobody detains me unless I want to be detained. There's no need at all for you to be angry with Franca.'

Were they going to discuss his fiancée for the entire journey? Leah's lips tightened. 'I'm not angry with Franca. I'm simply anxious to get on with what we came for.'

'I'm glad to hear it. In that case, you can stop scowling.' His tone, as he turned to her, was mockingly humorous. 'We ought to be there in about twenty minutes.'

They were there in less. Vincenzo pulled on the handbrake as they drew up outside his sister's pretty, secluded villa.

'This is it.' He reached for the door-handle. 'Now let's go and see if we can find them.'

To Leah's dismay no one answered the doorbell, and there was no car parked in the driveway or in the garage. In fact, there were no signs of life at all.

She made a tour of the building, tapping on the windows, while Vincenzo went off in search of neighbours. And all the while her heart was sinking inside her. It looked as though Jo and Carlo weren't here, after all.

'I've had a word with the people in the next villa.' Suddenly Vincenzo had reappeared. 'I've got good news and I've got bad news. Which do you want first?'

'The good news, please.' She crossed her fingers mentally. Perhaps it was possible that their excursion had not been a total waste of time.

'The good news is that they were here. They arrived a couple of days ago. The bad news is that I'm afraid we've just missed them. They've gone off somewhere for a couple of days.'

Leah clenched her fists. 'Off where?' she demanded.

'That I don't know. Apparently they didn't say. They just said they'd be back in a couple of days' time.'

A couple of days. Leah's heart sank. 'We've got to find them. Somehow, we've got to!'

'I don't see how we can. They could be anywhere. I think our best bet would be just to hang around until they reappear.'

'Hang around?' Leah ground the words at him. 'Maybe it suits you to hang around—no doubt you can amuse yourself with Franca while you're doing so!—but I'm afraid I'm taking this a lot more seriously. It might be too late by the time they get back. For all we know, they've gone off to get married!'

'For all we know, they have.' His expression had altered. There was a warning look deep at the back of his eyes. 'But I'm afraid there's nothing we can do about it.'

'There has to be!'

'Like what, for example?' His tone was gritty. 'Are we supposed to trail aimlessly around southern Italy when at any moment they might return here?

Use your common sense. That would just be stupid.'

Leah gasped with impatience. 'You *would* say that, wouldn't you? It suits you to hang around waiting at Franca's! Maybe that's the real reason that you came here—not to find Jo and Carlo at all, but just so you can spend a few nights in her bed!'

All at once his hands had taken hold of her, their grip like wire snares round her wrists. His eyes bored into her. 'What the hell's the matter with you? Have you taken complete leave of your senses?'

She felt as though she had. Her head was spinning. Suddenly all control over her emotions was slipping away from her.

Leah simply could not stop herself. 'Damn you!' she was spitting. 'You realise it's all your fault that we missed them? If you hadn't been so anxious to spend time with that woman, if we'd come straight here as I said we ought to, we probably could have arrived here in time!'

Her eyes sparked at him with unleashed fury. 'Couldn't you have restrained yourself for just a couple of hours longer? Or were you so utterly overcome with desire that you couldn't wait to get your hands on her?'

The fingers around her wrists had tightened. He shook her, stopping her in her tracks, silencing the shrill strident outburst.

'I really do think you've gone mad, *sposa mia*.' His voice was low and not angry as she had expected. He shook her again and pulled her to him, so that her body was pressed against his. 'I think you are the one with unfulfilled desires.' The black eyes surveyed her brightly flushed face, minutely, as though he could read every emotion. 'When was the last time you had a man in your bed? Is that your problem? Aren't you getting enough sex?'

Leah closed her eyes. Her whole body was trembling. Shame tore through her. Suddenly she felt sick.

'Is that it, *cara sposa*?' He held her, taunting her, his body hard and provocative against her, the scent of him singing in her nostrils. 'That must be hard for someone like yourself with such well-developed appetites of the flesh. No wonder the strain is proving too much for you.'

Leah breathed in deeply, but her head was still spinning. She wanted to lean against him to recover her equilibrium, yet at the same time, had she strength, she would have torn herself free.

She shook her head weakly. 'Let me go,' she pleaded. She took another deep breath. 'Please let me go.'

'Perhaps I can do something to alleviate your frustration?' He leaned towards her, suddenly very close. She could feel his breath against her face. 'After all, as you yourself were so eager to point out, you and I are still legally man and wife.'

'Please don't.' She was dying. Of humiliation and horror. Though there was another emotion, even more lethal, that was coiling inside her, threatening to strangle her.

She really had taken leave of her senses. As her eyes fell on the scar on his upper lip, she was seized with an absurd desire to kiss him.

'Don't what?' He had suddenly released her wrists and with one free hand had circled her waist. The other came up to slide into her hair, sending helpless shivers across her scalp. 'Don't what?' he repeated softly. 'Tell me, *sposa mia.*'

'Vincenzo, please.' Her eyes frowned into his face. She wanted to pull herself away, to demand that he release her instantly. But even more she longed to raise her lips to his.

'Is this what you don't want me to do?'

His eyes poured into hers for a long endless moment, their expression so intense that she could feel herself drowning. Then he was leaning a little closer, his arms tightening around her, and she felt her head lift up to meet him as his lips came down on hers at last.

It was just like that first time all those aching years ago. Inside her her heart seemed to open like a flower, reaching up to embrace the sun. A sudden bright warmth seemed to fill her being. Her blood was rushing, singing, through her veins.

'Vincenzo...'

'*Si, cara? Dimmi.*' Tell me. 'Tell me anything you want to.'

She shook her head helplessly. '*Niente.*' Her arms twined around his neck. 'Nothing. Just kiss me.'

'*Volentieri.*' Willingly. She felt him smile. Then his arms tightened around her and once more his lips sought hers.

She had forgotten how powerful his kisses could be. How sensuous, how erotic, how skin-tinglingly delicious. His lips seemed to tease her, making her breath catch, uttering unspoken promises of richer pleasures to come.

Her fingers laced his hair, her body pressing against him, alight with the memory of past promises fulfilled. She felt herself shudder. Her memory had not betrayed her. Nobody could love her like Vincenzo.

The lips that devoured her were the lips of an angel, carrying her soul and her senses to heaven. One minute soft and gently seductive, peppering her face with tiny scorching kisses, then a moment later, fierce with driven passion, the same lips threatened to consume her.

Her blood leapt within her as her own lips responded, parting eagerly, her tongue flicking against his tongue. And her fingers in his hair with greedy urgency sought to draw his lips more firmly against her. Vincenzo! Vincenzo! She could not stop it. His name was thundering inside her brain.

The fingers in her hair were sliding to her nape, sending shivers of electricity darting down her spine. Then they were caressing her shoulders, the back of her neck, then sweeping down towards her waist to curl around the edge of her T-shirt.

Leah's breath stopped within her. Her stomach turned to water. Suddenly every nerve-end in her body was on fire.

She felt him gently raise the T-shirt, then his hand grazed her nakedness as it moved unhurriedly towards her breast. She let out a gasp as his fingers reached her bra strap and gently but firmly pulled it down over her shoulder. Then he was peeling the bra from her aching, hardening flesh and cupping her breast in the palm of his hand.

'Che bella!' she heard him murmur against her face.

She closed her eyes and pressed against him. 'Oh, Vincenzo, Vincenzo!' she breathed.

And suddenly the ache in her loins was unbearable as he strummed the taut nipple with the flat of his thumb. Squeezing, teasing, making her blood burn. Every inch of her suddenly throbbed with the need for him.

She could sense that his own need was equally urgent. The hips that were pressed against her own were hard and hungry with desire. Through her skirt she could feel his swollen manhood.

His lips nuzzled her hair. 'Let's go inside.' His voice was hoarse. 'I have the key.'

Leah raised her eyes to his, her stomach clenching. She longed to say yes, but something stopped her.

Cold common sense? A sudden rush of fear? The shameful realisation that she had already gone too far?

Her tongue stuck to her palate. She shook her head. 'I can't do that. No. Absolutely.'

There was a momentary pause, then he released her. 'I see.' His voice had suddenly grown cold. He took an abrupt step back. 'I suggest we get out of here.' Then he was turning and heading back to the car.

Leah took a moment to collect herself, suddenly overcome by a sense of pure horror. What had possessed her? How could she have behaved so? What on earth had triggered such an appalling display?

She jerked her spine straight and took a deep breath. Whatever had caused that inexplicable aberration, it was over, done with, and she had stopped in time. At least there was that much to be thankful for.

Then safely back on the cold rails of her control she headed down the path to where the car was parked. She pulled the door open and slid in without looking at him. 'I'm sorry about that. I don't know what got into me.'

'Sorry about what? About starting or about stopping?' His tone was taunting. 'I still have the key if you've changed your mind again.'

'I haven't changed my mind. Nor am I likely to. As I said, I don't know what got into me.'

'No, it wasn't like you—stopping halfway, I mean.' She felt him turn and rake her face with his eyes. 'But I think I can tell you what got into you.' There was a hard mocking smile in his voice as he added, 'You're hungry, *sposa mia*. Hungry for a man. That was a message I had no trouble at all deciphering.'

She swung round then to glare at him. 'How dare you?' she spluttered.

'Do you deny it?'

'I most certainly do!'

'So, there's a man in your life?'

'Absolutely!'

'Someone who satisfies you?'

'More than you could ever do!'

He simply smiled at the insult. 'I would never have suspected. I had the feeling you were leading a more solitary life these days.'

'And why should I be doing that? Do you think I'm incapable of finding someone else? Someone to love and spend my life with?'

'So, there's someone serious?'

'Extremely serious.' She was suddenly quite caught up in this lie she was spinning, almost as though she believed it herself. 'Someone I'm planning to marry, if you must know, just as soon as the divorce comes through.'

'Well, well.' Vincenzo nodded. 'My congratulations. I'm delighted for you. I hope you'll both be happy.' He switched on the engine. 'Oh, by the way... There was really no need for you to get so upset back there...'

As she frowned, he elaborated, 'About missing the errant lovers... You seemed to think it was all my fault, that if we'd come straight here we wouldn't have missed them.' He slid the gear-stick into first. 'You were wrong about that. The story is that they left early this morning, before you and I had even left Rome.'

Leah felt suddenly foolish, and annoyed with herself. What had happened back there could have been avoided. If she hadn't worked herself into such a passion of anger, one thing wouldn't have led to another and that unfortunate episode would never have occurred.

Vincenzo turned to glance at her, his dark eyes shuttered. 'I just thought I'd better make that clear. So we know where we stand—on every count. I wouldn't like us to get our wires crossed again.'

Then he thrust his foot down hard on the accelerator and, with an angry squeal of tyres, they set off down the road.

CHAPTER SEVEN

As THEY headed at speed along the motorway, the third act of *Rigoletto* blaring from the speakers, Leah took the opportunity to do a bit of quiet thinking.

What she had told Vincenzo, of course, had been a lie, but now that it was done she didn't regret it. After all, she rationalised, it could have been true. Though her relationship with the one and only man in her life—Ronald—was strictly platonic, he had hinted more than once that he would love for them to marry. And—who knew?—one day in the future she might consider doing so.

But the real reason she didn't regret the small inaccuracy was that she sensed it might have some value in her dealings with Vincenzo. Her supposed engagement set a boundary between them, a boundary that was becoming increasingly necessary. For, though all sentiment between them had expired years ago, it was clear that the ill-fated physical attraction, unfortunately, was very far from dead.

And though it was easy for her to swear in her saner moments that shameful episodes like this afternoon's must never be allowed to happen again, when the flames began to leap it wasn't so easy to douse them.

She slid a secret sidelong glance at Vincenzo, quelling the instant sharp twist in her stomach. His engagement to Franca ought to have been sufficient—if he had been the faithful kind, capable of sexual loyalty. Quite clearly he wasn't, as she had already known, anyway—so this invented engagement of hers was simply a double safety measure.

The tenor from *Rigoletto* was singing 'La donna è mobile'. Woman is fickle. That's what the words meant. Leah pulled a rueful face and mentally crossed her fingers. Whatever temptations fate might throw at her, she would not be unfaithful to her fantasy fiancé!

'So, what happens now?'

They had returned to Franca's villa and were having pre-dinner drinks out on the veranda. Dressed in another of her exquisite silk caftans, Franca draped herself elegantly against the stone balustrade. 'What happens now, *caro*?' she repeated, casting a seductive smile in Vincenzo's direction. 'Does this mean you'll be staying on here?'

'I'm afraid it does.' Vincenzo was seated in one of the armchairs, cradling a glass of whisky in his long, tanned fingers. 'We'll have to stay here until they come back. I hope you have no objection, *ciccia mia*?'

Leah squirmed inwardly at the sticky endearment and scowled down into her Cinzano and soda. Of course she doesn't mind, she thought with irritation, crossing her legs as she leaned back in her own chair. She's only too pleased to have you here!

But there was a surprise in store. Franca slid down from the balustrade and crossed sinuously to drape herself on the arm of Vincenzo's chair. 'Of course I don't mind. Stay here as long as you want to. But you're remembering that I have to go to Naples tomorrow? I have a little bit of business that I have to take care of.'

'Ah, yes. I'd forgotten.' He was smiling up at her. 'But do you think it's quite safe to leave me alone here with Leah? Without you to keep an eye on us, who knows what might happen?'

Sadistic swine! Leah glanced up then, feeling a sudden unexpected shaft of sympathy for Franca. Oh, he definitely hadn't changed! It still amused him to torture without mercy the woman who loved him.

She threw him a harsh look, then glanced at Franca. 'Nothing will happen,' she assured the other woman. Her tone was laced with enough distaste to make it clear that she would fight off any advances.

Franca merely smiled, not put out in the slightest. Clearly, she refused to consider for one moment the possibility that her fiancé might be capable of betraying her.

'Don't worry,' she answered. 'I know he was only joking. He's a man who respects the feelings of the woman he loves.'

Leah was saved the trouble of having to compose her features to disguise the sceptical smile she felt forming there, as at that very moment the maid appeared in the doorway.

Franca rose to her feet. 'Excuse me a moment. I see my presence is required in the kitchen.'

'You see what a high opinion she has of me?' As Franca disappeared, Vincenzo turned to toss a provocative glance across at Leah. 'Unlike you, *cara sposa mia*. For some reason you always preferred to believe the worst of me.' He paused and frowned lightly. 'How come you never trusted me?'

'Perhaps I was wiser. Perhaps I knew you better.'

'Or perhaps it was your guilty conscience?' he challenged. 'You assumed that I would be as unfaithful as you were.'

Leah swirled her glass a moment as she raised her eyes to look at him—looking cool and immaculate in a cream linen suit. Unconsciously, with coral-tipped fingers, she smoothed the skirt of her matching coral dress.

'I think your chronology is just a little off. You're the one who was unfaithful first.'

Vincenzo took a mouthful of his drink. 'Are you trying to tell me that that particular incident—the one we both know about—was the first?'

'The first and only.' She held his eyes and spoke calmly, though the fingers around her glass had tightened. Why did this subject still pain her so desperately? Would she ever be able to tell the truth? 'You're the one who went in for multiple conquests.'

In the past he had always denied it, but now he did not. After all, it was history. It no longer mattered. And besides, Leah thought cynically, he was saving his lies for Franca.

He sat back in his chair, long legs stretched out in front of him, as supple and as unrepentant as a cat. 'So, this fiancé of yours... Does he know all about his future's wife tendency to stray periodically?'

'This time there'll be no straying. Ronald's a different type of man. We have a different kind of relationship altogether.'

'So I gather.' Vincenzo smiled mockingly, making mute but unmistakable reference to the sexual hunger he had earlier accused her of. 'I'm surprised that sort of relationship agrees with you, *cara*.'

'Well, it does. For the moment. Later it will be different.' She cleared her throat. 'Later, when we're married.'

She had more or less admitted that he had been right, that her relationship with Ronald was totally celibate. That was OK. It was true, after all. But she was loath to admit a more revealing truth—that she had slept with no man since the day she had left Italy. There were all sorts of ways in which he might misinterpret that.

She smiled a half-smile, almost conspiratorial. 'Ronald's a little old-fashioned in these matters. Abstinence isn't my way, as you know, and it presents for me something of an unusual situation. But I love him and I respect his wishes.'

'How very commendable.' His eyes narrowed a little. 'What a pity you weren't so conscientious about respecting *my* wishes. After all, they were rather less demanding. All I asked was that my wife be faithful.'

Leah's heart squeezed painfully. She forced herself to look at him. 'You didn't deserve a faithful wife.'

'Because of my multiple conquests, as you call them?' He raised one dark eyebrow. 'Is that the reason?'

That as well. But it was not what she had been meaning. He had deserved her infidelity because he had never loved her. He had deserved to suffer— for at least his pride had suffered—for the calculating way that he had used her.

But she was saved the anguish of having to answer him, as Franca, displaying perfect timing, came sweeping through the french doors on to the terrace to rejoin them.

She clapped her hands. 'Drink up!' she beamed cheerfully. 'Dinner will be served in ten minutes!'

Dinner, for Leah, was even more uncomfortable than lunch. The food was exquisite, as she had expected. A delicious seafood starter, followed by veal cutlets in a mouth-watering herb and mushroom sauce. Then fruit and a huge bowl of *tiramisu*—a lethal local dessert, rich with cream and liqueur and chocolate—with cheese and coffee and brandy to finish.

'That was absolutely fantastic.' Leah felt obliged to be polite, as she folded her napkin and smiled across at her hostess. 'Absolutely the best meal I've had in ages.'

'I'm glad you enjoyed it. But you've been so quiet! You're not feeling unwell, are you?' Franca mimicked concern.

'No, I'm feeling fine.' Leah mimicked a smile back at her. 'I'm sorry if I'm not being a very good guest.'

'You're being a charming guest! Absolutely charming! Perhaps you're just a little bit tired.' She pushed back her coffee-cup and stretched her arms above her head. 'Talking of tired, you must forgive me... I'm now going to be a terrible hostess and take myself off instantly to bed. I have to be up very early tomorrow morning.'

'*Povera Franca.*' Vincenzo murmured his sympathy. Poor Franca. He smiled at her, as she rose from the table. 'Are you really leaving us so soon?'

'I'm afraid so, *caro.*' She stooped to kiss his head and let her hands lightly mould his shoulders. Then it seemed to Leah that she raised her eyes for a moment, as though to make certain that she had her attention, before adding in a whisper what sounded like an invitation, 'Goodnight, *caro mio.* I'll see you when I see you.'

Leah felt it again then, that shaft of irritation that had been twisting at her insides periodically all evening. And as Franca ruffled his hair now and stole another glance at Leah, a self-satisfied smile curling round her lips, Leah found herself wondering with a flare of annoyance if this display of affection was partly for her benefit.

Was Franca warning her off? she wondered, glancing back at her. If she was, she could have saved herself the trouble. The only intention Leah harboured regarding Vincenzo was to cut and run the moment that was possible.

At last Franca withdrew and she was left alone with Vincenzo.

'Franca's right. You were quiet tonight. Do you have something on your mind. Are you worried about your sister?' Vincenzo poured more brandy into each of their glasses and sat back in his seat, eyeing her curiously.

Leah was suddenly wishing that she'd left with their hostess. She wasn't sure if she was up to another discussion with Vincenzo.

'Naturally I'm worried,' she answered without looking at him. In fact, she hadn't thought about Jo all evening.

'I'm curious to meet your sister. She was just a kid last time I saw her. Now that she's grown up, what's she like? Does she look like you?'

Some said she did. She had the same bright hair, the same blue eyes, the same independent spirit. Leah raised her eyes briefly. 'No. She's much prettier.'

'Impossible!' He laughed and fingered his brandy glass. 'No one could be more beautiful than you are. You are even more beautiful than you were five years ago.'

Leah hated the way her blood leapt at the compliment. She glared at him beneath her lashes. 'Beautiful, but fatally flawed,' she reminded him. 'At least my sister doesn't have any defects.'

He smiled at that. 'Who knows?' he murmured. 'Perhaps such weaknesses are in the blood.' He took a mouthful of his drink. 'Though, come to think of it, your mother is a charming and irreproachable woman. How is she these days? Does she still live in Guildford?'

What was all this sudden interest in her family? Leah scowled at him irritably. 'Why do you ask?'

'Just curious, that's all.' He smiled smoothly, sitting back in his seat and cradling his glass in one hand. 'And how does your mother feel about Jo's liaison with Carlo? Is she as horrified as her elder daughter?'

'She would be if she knew. I haven't told her. Since I intend to put a stop to it, I saw no need to upset her unnecessarily.'

'How extremely praiseworthy. I see you've matured. Once you would not have been so thoughtful.'

Leah felt a stab of guilt, remembering the tears and the trauma when she had announced to her mother that she had left Vincenzo. Her mother's pain at the failure of the marriage had been almost as great as Leah's.

And whose fault had all that been? she thought with sudden rancour. Suddenly she'd had quite enough of this conversation.

She straightened a little. 'Please don't feel obliged to sit here with me and make polite conversation. I know you're not the least bit interested in my family.' She paused a brief moment, her eyes hardening as she looked at him. 'Why don't you just excuse yourself and go and join Franca? I won't mind in the least and I'm sure she's chafing for your company.'

'You might be right.' He smiled amusedly. 'But do you mind terribly if I finish my brandy first?'

Leah continued to look at him, eyes unblinking. 'Why not take it with you as a kind of *aperitif*?'

He smiled at that. 'Not a bad idea.' Then he lifted one eyebrow and raised his glass to his lips, savouring the brandy, letting it roll round his mouth. 'That was one of the little vices we shared, as I recall—having a glass of wine in bed before making love.'

'Was it?' She had to fight to keep her cheeks from flaming. That light in his eye was the same sensuous light that, once, could reduce her limbs to jelly. 'It was such a long time ago. I really don't recall.'

'I take it you don't go in for such indulgences these days?' He smiled suddenly, letting his dark eyes roam over her. 'No. Of course. I was forgetting. This fiancé of yours... What's his name? Ronald? He rather cramps your style.'

'He doesn't cramp my style in the slightest.' She had a sudden vivid flash of those times they'd spent together in the big double bed at the Villa Petruzzi, drinking pink champagne as a prelude to making love. She felt an emptiness within her. Those days had been special. Crazy and exciting. There had been nothing like it since.

Leah took a deep breath. 'It was you who cramped my style. All you ever did for me was waste a year of my life.'

Vincenzo drained his glass. His smile had died a little. There was a momentary firming of the lines around his mouth.

'Happy memories.' He held her gaze a moment, and there was something in his eyes that made Leah look away. A soft look, even wistful, was how she once might have described it. And she had forgotten how that look could make her die of love for him. Even now, after all this time, it pulled at her heartstrings.

He was rising to his feet. 'Very well. Since you insist, I'll take my leave now. I wish you goodnight and pleasant dreams.'

Leah met his eyes briefly. 'Goodnight,' she answered. Suddenly she couldn't wait for him to leave. Her heart was thumping like a fist against her ribcage.

'Ah, I was almost forgetting...' As he was about to move away, Vincenzo paused and reached across the table. 'That idea of yours really rather appeals to me.' He unstoppered the brandy decanter and poured a generous measure. More than enough for two, Leah observed.

'Thanks for reminding me.' He raised the glass briefly, his eyes dancing, enjoying the way he was mocking her. 'Once more, goodnight.' He turned on his heel. 'I'll see you some time in the morning.'

Leah did not answer. She watched him go in silence, wondering why this emptiness inside her was growing and why she suddenly felt an almost irrepressible desire to drop her head in her hands and weep.

Franca had already left when Leah awoke next morning, and Vincenzo had gone down to the sea for a swim. She spotted him when she threw back the shutters of her bedroom window, cutting his way cleanly through the crushed-diamond water.

She stared at him for a moment, her heart reacting strangely, thumping with a dull beat in her chest. I wish I didn't hate him, she thought with sudden passion. I wish I was capable of feeling nothing at all.

She sighed and turned away. That day would come some day. Then, finally and for ever, she would be free.

Breakfast was served out on the terrace, with its magnificent view out over the beach and the sea. What a beautiful place to live, Leah pondered, gazing round her. No wonder Franca was reluctant to leave it.

She bit into her croissant, crispy-warm and spread with butter. If only the poor woman knew what she was getting into, perhaps she would do the wise thing and just stay where she was. Marriage to Vincenzo, she would soon discover, was a thankless state, full of frustration and pain.

Talk of the devil! As she glanced up suddenly, he was striding across the beach, heading for the veranda.

'Good morning!' he greeted her. 'So, you've finally surfaced.' A moment later he was standing by the table. 'You don't mind if I join you for a coffee?'

'Good morning.' Leah glanced up at him, then glanced away quickly, averting her eyes like some untouched virgin from the arresting vision of his semi-naked form.

He wore nothing but swimming-trunks, with a towel draped round his neck, and his body was as lean and dark and powerful as Leah remembered it from the old days.

She was aware that he had noticed her reaction. She could sense the smile that curled round his lips. Instantly she hurried to cover her tracks and enquired politely, though she wasn't really interested, 'Well, did you enjoy your swim?'

'My swim was excellent. Most invigorating.' He wiped a droplet of water from his chin with the towel and pushed his fingers through his wet black hair. 'But there are a lot of nasty currents out there. Bear that in mind if you decide to have a swim yourself.'

Then to Leah's dismay he began to sit down, stretching his long legs out under the table, brushing her knee briefly with one hard-muscled thigh.

She felt her heart leap like a startled frog inside her. All at once her hands felt hot and clammy.

The realisation appalled her. Was it really possible that that brief contact with his naked body could have had such an instantaneous effect on her? Was the sexual allure of him really still so powerful?

It was a galling admission but the answer was yes.

She sought refuge in outrage and fixed her eyes on his face. 'I don't really think you're dressed for the table. Don't you think you ought to go and put something on first?'

'Does my naked state upset you?' He pulled his chair closer. 'Changed days, eh, *sposa mia*? It never used to.'

Leah pursed her lips. 'It doesn't upset me. I simply find it a trifle tasteless.'

He smiled at that. She could hardly blame him. 'This fiancé of yours has really got to you.' He poured coffee and helped himself to sugar. 'It sounds to me as though he's not a lot of fun.'

Leah bit into her croissant and threw him a cool look. 'He doesn't have to be fun. He's honest and he's decent. And, what's more, he loves me. That's what really counts.'

'And you love him?'

'Would I marry him if I didn't? Surely that wouldn't be very honest.'

A long look passed between them that spoke a thousand words. They both knew that for Leah love was a prerequisite to marriage, and, equally, they both knew that for Vincenzo it wasn't.

Vincenzo turned away and glanced down into his coffee, fiddling with the silver coffee-spoon with long tanned fingers. 'While we're on the subject of love and marriage...' His eyes sought hers, their expression mocking. 'I took a quick run out to Paluro before breakfast. It would appear that the lovebirds haven't returned yet.'

'You went without me?' It was an accusation. 'You'd no business doing that. We agreed to confront them together.'

'I went without you because you were still in bed.'

Leah glared at him impatiently. 'You could have wakened me,' she challenged.

He shook his head. 'Sorry, that's not my job.' All at once there was an alligator bite in his voice. 'I'm not employed as your personal wake-up service.'

'Then you could have waited until I got up. Surely there was no need to go quite so early?'

'It was convenient for me to go early.' His eyes bored through her. 'If it wasn't convenient for you, I'm afraid that's your problem.'

'I see. So this is how it's going to be? Everything's got to be done your way, without any consultation with me?'

He smiled a taunting smile. 'Consultation? What's that? I'm afraid it's not a word that figures in my vocabulary.'

'No, it doesn't, does it?' She could feel her anger boiling, and, though she knew that he was deliberately baiting her, somehow she couldn't manage to bite her anger back. 'Don't you ever get tired of being so damned selfish? Don't you ever get bored with only ever thinking of yourself?'

He shrugged infuriatingly and reached for a croissant, bit into it and chewed thoughtfully before answering, 'Boredom isn't something I ever suffer from, so I suppose the answer to that must be negative.'

Leah counted to ten. She felt like hitting him. She felt like ramming the croissant down his throat. 'It's a way of life to you, selfishness, isn't it? I wonder if you've ever performed an unselfish act?'

'I dare say I have—in a moment of inattention.' He smiled with dry amusement. 'We all make mistakes.'

It was no good. She knew from past experience that she could never get the better of him when he was in a mood like this. She tossed down her napkin and rose stiffly to her feet. 'I'm going down to the beach for a while. If you decide to go to Paluro, please let me know. I'd like to be included this time.'

He did not answer. His eyes looked right through her as he popped the rest of the croissant into his mouth.

Leah turned away angrily. Lord, how she hated him! I hope you choke on that damned croissant! she muttered to herself.

Ten minutes later, down on the beach, her anger was still burning like hot rods inside her. She slipped off her beach dress and sát down on the sunbed, adjusting the straps of her coral-pink bikini, flipped open her tube of sun-cream and proceeded to slap some on.

I might have known he'd take the law into his own hands! she fumed silently. When did he ever do anything different? She flicked back her hair as she smoothed cream on her shoulders. And what would have happened if Jo and Carlo had been there? Knowing him, the confrontation would have been a disaster. He probably would have ended up triggering the calamity that both of them were hoping to avoid!

She took a deep breath. From now on she must be vigilant. She must make sure he didn't cut her out again.

But for the moment, in the meantime... She sank on to her back, feeling the warmth of the sun embrace her like a mantle. For the moment she would relax and put him from her mind. It did no good at all to get wound up like this.

'How's the suntan coming along?'

She had barely settled when he was standing there beside her, looking down at her, towering over the sunbed.

Leah shot him a glance of naked disapproval. 'It's coming along fine, thank you, *without* your assistance.' Perhaps he would take the hint and leave her alone.

And pigs might fly! He squatted on the sand alongside her. 'The sun's pretty hot. I hope you're well protected? I wouldn't like to see that pretty skin of yours get sunburnt.'

There he was again, taking control, trying to lay down the law, as though it was his divine right to do so!

Leah felt her blood begin to boil again. 'I assure you there's really no need for you to concern yourself.' The words issued like a hiss from between clenched teeth. 'I'd be grateful if you'd just leave me alone.'

'With your fair skin you need to take care.' He ignored her request and stretched his long frame more comfortably. 'Now Franca and me, we're a different story. We're used to all this sunshine. We've been brought up to it.'

So, now she was to be subjected to a cosy little lecture on all the things that he and Franca had in common!

Leah had suddenly reached her limit. She sprang up from the sunbed and, without looking at him, announced, 'I'm going for a swim.'

Then she was running towards the shoreline, across foot-scorching sand, and wading gratefully into the shallows, cool gentle eddies foaming around her ankles.

The water felt delicious. She threw herself in. Then she was striking out towards the horizon, the strength of her anger propelling her forward. All she wanted was to get as far away as possible from that wretched man who was driving her mad.

At last she slowed down, her fury finally dissipated, and rolled over on to her back to float for a while. The sky above her blazed like an enormous sapphire. A cool breeze fanned her limbs. She closed her eyes.

It was heaven. Just floating. Thinking of nothing. I could stay like this all day, she thought blissfully.

But then she opened her eyes and turned over lazily, intending to swim another few strokes. And suddenly she frowned. Where on earth was she? That wasn't the beach she had started out from.

In the very same instant, as she let her legs drop, something was tugging at her ankles. Furiously, she kicked, as though to free herself, but the tugging grew stronger. She began to go under.

That was when she panicked, her arms flailing the water. She managed to cry, 'Help!' before she went under again. And, too late, she was remembering Vincenzo's warning about the currents.

I'm going to drown, she thought helplessly, as she went under for the third time.

CHAPTER EIGHT

LEAH opened her eyes and blinked up at the sun. 'What happened? Where am I?' She felt dizzy and faint.

'You're all right. I'm here with you.'

Dimly, she could make out the shadowy figure of Vincenzo. He was leaning over her, smoothing back her hair. And his voice, like her own, seemed to come from far away.

'Did you save me?' she murmured. She found it difficult to talk. 'I was drowning... The currents... They were dragging me under...'

'You're all right now. Just relax, *amore mio*.'

As she closed her eyes again, her head spinning strangely, she felt him scoop her limp body gently from the sand and lift her up into his arms.

How safe she felt, how protected from the world. No one but Vincenzo had ever made her feel like that. She let her head fall lightly against his shoulder. 'Thank you,' she murmured. 'You saved my life.'

Leah was scarcely aware of the short trek across the beach. She seemed to be drifting in and out of consciousness. The next thing she knew Vincenzo was laying her on a sofa and pulling a warm blanket up around her shoulders.

'Don't move,' he told her. 'I'm going to call a doctor. And then I'll make you something hot to drink.'

'That's really not necessary. I'm perfectly OK.' The protest was automatic. She hated to be a bother. 'Really,' she insisted. 'I'll be fine in a minute.'

In response he simply smiled. 'I'll be the judge of that.' He tucked the soft blanket more firmly beneath her chin. 'So kindly stop arguing and just stay where you are.'

She didn't have much choice, Leah thought with a wry smile, as he turned on his heel and strode out of the room. She had the very distinct feeling that if she'd tried to stand up her legs would not have been able to hold her. She sighed and leaned her head against the cushions. What a fool she'd been. She'd forgotten about the currents.

It seemed only a moment later that Vincenzo reappeared, dressed now in jeans and a loosely open shirt and carrying a mug of sweet black coffee.

'Here. Drink this.' He eased her up into a sitting position, one arm firm about her shoulders, and raised the mug up to her lips. 'Just sip it,' he urged as she tried to take a mouthful. 'Nice and easy. Don't try to hurry it.'

Then, at last, when she'd drunk half, he laid the cup aside and settled her once more against the cushions. He pushed back her hair, which by now was almost dry, and seated himself on the sofa beside her. 'I managed to get hold of Franca's doctor. He said he'd be here in about half an hour.'

She had been about to protest again, for already she was feeling better. Her head had stopped spinning and her limbs felt less shaky. But as she looked into his face, her heart stopped for a moment. All at once she was filled with a bitter-sweet memory.

It was not the first time she had seen this side of Vincenzo. This gentleness, this protectiveness, this firm gentle caring. In the early days he had behaved like this to her often, easing her passage from child to woman, from uncertain adolescent to wife. And neither was it the first time that he had come to her rescue at a moment when she needed him desperately. And that other time was etched for ever in her memory.

It had been when her father had died from his second heart attack, just a brief few months after their wedding. His kindness to her then had been overwhelming. Endless. Untiring. She would never forget it.

Tears of emotion suddenly sprang to her eyes. Tears for her father. Tears for Vincenzo. Tears for all the sadness there had been.

'*Amore mio.*' He reached for her instantly, wrapping his arms like a warm cloak around her. One hand held her head, stroking her hair gently. 'Cry if you want to. It might make you feel better.' His lips brushed her hair, his breath warm against her scalp. 'You've had a shock. No wonder you're upset.'

She had wanted to pull back, but instead she leaned against him, letting her cheek rest lightly against his chest. For some reason it felt perfectly natural to do so. It would have made no sense to resist.

Yet she felt vulnerable like this. Her heart was beating strangely. She took a deep breath and sought to exchange rationality for emotion. 'How did you know I'd got into trouble? You must have been watching me from the beach.'

'Fortunately, I was—though I thought you were fine at first. It was only when I noticed how far you'd drifted that I realised you were unaware of the currents.'

Leah pulled a face. 'In spite of your warning.'

But he did not pick up on this opening to chastise her. Instead, he continued, 'You were already losing consciousness by the time I got to you. I towed you back to shore as quickly as possible and subjected you to a bit of mouth-to-mouth resuscitation.'

He drew her head back and smiled at her amusedly. 'I do hope you'll forgive me for taking such liberties?'

Leah felt her cheeks pink. Then she smiled at him wryly. 'Weren't you tempted just to let me drown? After all, you keep saying that I'm nothing but trouble.'

He did not answer for an instant, just frowned a little as he looked into her face. His eyes, as black as midnight, were remote and unreadable.

'No,' he said at last. 'Not even for a moment.' With his thumb he dried her cheek where a tear had fallen, sending a warm sensation wriggling through her. Then he half smiled. 'As tempting as that might have been from a purely personal point of view, think of all the inconvenience it would have caused when the body of a beautiful young English girl was finally washed up on the beach.' He pulled a face. 'I knew it would have been more trouble than it was worth.'

He was only joking. Leah knew that. And it was she who'd put the idea into his head. As something twisted inside her, she wished she hadn't. For some foolish reason his harmless jest had hurt.

'More coffee?' He was reaching once more for the cup and pulling the blanket around her shoulders as she shifted away from him and leaned back against the cushions.

She nodded and reached out to take the cup from his hand before he could raise it to her lips. 'I'll manage,' she assured him. 'I'm feeling much better.'

The doctor's visit was reassuringly brief. 'You're perfectly fine now, but your system's had a shock. Best take it easy for a couple of hours—then see how you feel. Just play it by ear.'

'I'll take you for a drive,' Vincenzo decided, once the doctor had gone and Leah was back on her feet again. 'I'll show you a bit of the surrounding countryside and we can stop off somewhere and have a leisurely lunch.'

It sounded a good idea. Leah nodded. 'Let's stop off first at Paluro, just to make sure that they haven't showed up.'

She almost hadn't said it. Mention of Paluro seemed likely to embitter the atmosphere between them, and she was finding their current truce agreeable and pleasant.

But Vincenzo simply shrugged. 'Of course. If you want to. It'll only take us a couple of minutes.' Perhaps he too was grateful for the truce—or perhaps he was simply being kind to her after the accident.

At any rate their visit to Paluro proved fruitless. The lovebirds, as Vincenzo called them, were still away. But for once, as they turned around and headed for the coast road, Leah felt grateful that their efforts had drawn a blank. She was not much in the mood for a confrontation today and it was a huge relief to have been spared such an ordeal.

Not, she hurried to assure herself, because of herself and Vincenzo and this mellow interlude they were enjoying. That, though pleasant, was of no real significance and was bound to be disrupted sooner or later anyway. The reason, she decided, leaning back in her seat, was simply that she was in need of a bit of tranquillity. She had already suffered more than enough trauma for one day.

The scenery along the Campania coast road was spectacular. The sea shimmering beneath a cloudless sky on one side, and on the other the hills peaked with deep green cypresses and dotted with pretty villages twinkling in the sun.

'I know just the place to have lunch.' Vincenzo winked across at her as he turned off the main road. 'It's a little hilltop village. I know you'll love it.'

Leah smiled across at him. 'If you say so.' And as she gazed for a moment upon his handsome dark profile, she felt an oddly familiar sensation inside her. This reminded her of the early days of their marriage when he would whisk her off to unexpected places, surprising and delighting her in equal measure with his endless spontaneity and sense of fun.

They had been wonderful days.

She glanced away quickly, stifling the unexpected sense of loss that flared inside her. She was being sentimental and, more to the point, foolish. The only reason those days had been wonderful was because she had not yet learned the truth about him.

But these bitter thoughts fled a moment later as the winding hilly road suddenly opened into a pretty piazza in the centre of the village.

'This is it.' Vincenzo pulled on the handbrake. 'Our restaurant is just over there.'

It was a typical little family-run trattoria, noisy and bustling, the tables all crammed together, and full of delicious mouth-watering aromas. They were shown to an al fresco table on the terrace, shaded by huge bright sun-umbrellas and with a spectacular view out over the sea.

Leah grinned delightedly. 'You're right, I love it.' And, to add to its appeal, quite suddenly, she was starving. 'I think I'm going to enjoy myself here!'

Predictably, the food was divine. Home-made pasta in a tantalising sauce, delicious seafood, excellent wine. Then pudding, cheese and fruit—almost more than they could cope with.

It was as they were enjoying a leisurely cup of coffee that Leah let her eyes drift out to sea, then on a sudden impulse she glanced back to ask him,

'Do you still have your yacht?'

Over the past couple of hours they had chatted non-stop—about Leah's new career as a textile designer, about the various developments at Petruzzi Automobili, about holidays they'd had and new friends they'd made. About everything, in fact, except the past.

And the yacht was the past. It was where they'd spent their honeymoon. Just for a moment a look passed between them.

'Yes, I still have it.' His gaze flickered briefly. Annoyance? Leah wondered, wondering also why

she'd said it. It had not been her intention to raise
spectres between them. It was simply that the
question had popped into her head.

'Do you use it much?' She wanted to change the
subject, but at the same time she felt trapped by
her own thoughtless folly. And, besides, she was
reluctant to retreat too fast and thereby reveal her
sudden discomfort.

'I use it a fair bit.' He did not seem discomfited,
but there was a sudden shuttered look about his
eyes. 'As you know, it's an ideal place for entertaining friends.'

She had an instant vision of Franca standing elegantly on the poop deck, her bright silk caftan
billowing in the breeze. And to her utter dismay a
knife twisted inside her. Foolish resentment. And
worse. Shameful jealousy.

As she sought to swallow it, Vincenzo smiled
suddenly. 'Have you done any sailing since you left
Italy? I seem to remember you were a damned good
sailor.'

'Unfortunately, I haven't.' Was Franca a good
sailor? The question pricked at her as she sought
to compose herself. 'I really haven't had much
opportunity.'

'That's a pity.' He drank back his coffee. Then
he threw her a wink. 'If you're feeling up to it, we
could hire a catamaran and go for a sail this afternoon. I promise you I'll do all the hard work.'

It was a splendid idea. Leah's humour changed
instantly. She smiled gratefully across at him. 'I'd
absolutely love to!'

'OK, but first a nice long walk to help digest this
enormous lunch we've just had.' He beckoned the

waiter and asked for the bill. Then, 'Come on,' he urged Leah. 'I'll show you round the village.'

To her delight Leah had lost none of her flair for sailing. And in the event she more than pulled her weight, setting the sails and adjusting the rigging, as the tiny twin-hulled vessel skimmed across the waves.

'That was terrific! I enjoyed every minute!' She was beaming with pleasure as they climbed ashore at last and headed back across the beach towards the car. The truth was she hadn't enjoyed herself so much for a long time. She felt positively effervescent, bubbling over with vitality.

Vincenzo smiled as he unlocked the passenger door. 'I'm glad you enjoyed it. You look terrific. A couple of hours on the high seas evidently agrees with you.'

What agrees with me is the excitement of your company. The thought flashed into her head unbidden. She turned away abruptly and climbed into the passenger-seat. Was she out of her mind to think such a thing?

She held her breath and deliberately did not look at him, as a moment later he climbed in beside her. Suddenly his nearness made her feel claustrophobic, emotionally as well as physically. He filled the space beside her and the space within her. At that moment he was her heartbeat and every thought in her head.

Almost desperately she turned to look at him. 'Suddenly I'm tired. Let's go back to the villa at once,' she said.

Gripped by sudden panic, she longed to escape him, to retreat to her room, to close the door and windows and drive him from her mind.

But he was smiling. 'Good idea. And, since you're feeling tired, I shall cook dinner for us tonight. It's the maid's evening off, but I'm in the mood anyway. You can put your feet up and watch, if you like.'

I want to go to bed. The thought of spending the evening together appalled her. But before she could protest he had switched on some music. 'Now just sit back and relax,' he commanded. 'We'll be back at the villa before you know it.'

By the time they got back she had calmed down a little. There's no harm in an innocent dinner together, she decided. And, besides, she'd been enjoying herself—as he had, too, she sensed. A pleasant meal together would round off the day.

It was only in the very depths of her heart that she admitted the real reason she was about to succumb to his wishes was that in the mood he was in—warm, seductive and carefree—it quite simply was not within her power to resist him.

Leah had forgotten what an excellent cook Vincenzo was—and how he tended to exaggerate on the size of the portions.

'There's enough here for an army!' she teased him, laughing, as he produced yet another dish of goodies to add to the array laid out on the table. 'It'll take us a week to get through this lot!'

In fact, to the surprise of both of them, most of it got eaten.

'It was that sailing that did it,' Vincenzo proclaimed, pushing aside his fruit plate at last. 'All that exercise gave us an appetite.'

'It also had a lot to do with the skill of the chef.' She smiled across at him. He deserved the compliment. 'I must say you haven't lost your touch.'

'That's nice to know.' His dark eyes fixed her, their expression oddly intimate, causing her to blush.

But she did not snatch her gaze away. She continued to look back at him. 'Did you ever really think you might have?' she challenged.

Even to her own ears the question sounded ambiguous. And in truth she was uncertain what she'd really meant by it. All she knew was that suddenly she felt a little bit reckless.

He had laid aside his napkin and was rising to his feet. And Leah knew exactly what he was going to do next.

His dark eyes still fixing her, he walked slowly round the table and came to stand right next to her chair. Then he took her by the hand and drew her to her feet. 'Shall we have coffee here or on the terrace?'

It was an irrelevant question. He was not thinking of coffee. She could see that in his eyes. And neither was she.

She let her eyes roam his face, a sudden excitement within her, and, as he smiled, her gaze drifted down to his mouth. Her heart turned over. The breath caught within her. Without a word she raised her free hand to touch the scar on his lip.

'It's almost faded away now.' He was still smiling as he said it. The hand that held hers seemed to tighten a little.

'Almost, but not quite. It'll never fade entirely. It'll always be there to remind us,' she answered.

His free hand touched her cheek, softly caressing. 'Surely by now you've forgotten all of that?'

Leah looked into his eyes. 'I'll never forget. How could I?' Her heart quivered. 'I thought you would die.'

As she said it, she felt once more that sense of stark horror that she had felt that rainy afternoon five years ago when she'd received that dreadful phone call from the hospital. He'd been down at the test track, testing the company's new car, when on a bend he'd skidded and gone out of control. He was in Intensive Care, unconscious, badly injured.

'Brace yourself,' the doctor had told her. 'There's a strong possibility that he may not survive.'

The weeks that had followed had been a nightmare. She had never left his bedside. She had never stopped praying. For she had known that without him she would not want to go on living. Without Vincenzo there would be nothing to live for.

'But I didn't die, did I?' He brought her back to the present. 'Thanks to your prayers, I made it in the end.'

Leah shook her head, her gaze once more on his mouth. She had believed that scar to be a kind of talisman. A reminder that fate had saved him for her and a promise that it always would.

She snatched her gaze away now and looked up into his eyes. 'You're crazy, you know, to go on test-driving those cars of yours. Why do you want to go on risking your life?'

His fingers stroked her cheek. 'Perhaps those prayers of yours are still working. Perhaps that's why I'm still here to tell the tale.' Then as she frowned, he smiled softly. 'Don't worry about it. I promise you, I don't take risks.'

'But how on earth can you avoid taking risks, hurtling round that awful test-track at heaven knows how many kilometres an hour?'

She was about to say more, but he laid a finger on her lips, and for a long endless moment he looked into her eyes. 'Be silent, *sposa mia*. Just kiss me,' he whispered.

The touch of his finger sent a warm shiver through her. She felt her lips part eagerly as his eyes consumed her. Then, as naturally as breathing, she raised her hands to his shoulders and let them slide up into the silky black hair.

She closed her eyes and let her body fall against him as his arms circled her waist, his hands pressed against her back.

'Kiss me!' he murmured hoarsely once more against her face. Then, as his lips came down on hers, her heart responded, 'Yes!'

It was a sweet kiss, so sweet she felt it must kill her. Her limbs had grown weak. Her heart was pounding. His kiss was like a drug, carrying her away.

'Leah... Cara Leah...'

She could feel his heart pounding, beat for beat, in frantic time with her own. And through the sweetness of his kiss a fire crackled between them, drawing them together into its flames. Leah could feel it licking at her senses, scorching at her nerve-ends, igniting the blood that pounded in her veins.

And she knew where it was leading her. She had been there often. And she longed for that destination with every fibre of her soul.

She offered no resistance as he gathered her to him and very gently lifted her up into his arms. She simply clung to him more tightly and buried her face against him, drinking in the sweet familiar scent of him, as on brisk strides he carried her out of the room, across the hall and up the stairs.

Then he was pushing a door open, then closing it again behind them. And suddenly her heart was beating uncontrollably. The noise of it deafened her and filled the whole room.

As he laid her on the bed, her arms were round his neck, drawing him alongside her, her lips reaching for his. And as he kissed her and caressed her, she could feel the hunger in him. And she loved the feel of it. It felt as powerful as her own.

With burning fingers he was reaching for her T-shirt, peeling it in one movement over her head, while her own fingers were fumbling impatiently with his shirt buttons, her face pressed against his chest, breathing in his naked flesh.

'Cara mia bella . . .'

He was kissing her shoulders, his urgency growing as he shrugged off his shirt and pulled her skirt down over her hips. Then she felt her stomach clench as with one impatient movement he reached round to unhook the fastening of her bra so that her breasts spilled excitedly against him.

A shuddering sigh escaped her. 'Oh, Vincenzo...!'

His eyes swept over her. '*Sei bella!* You're so beautiful!' Then he was leaning over her, his hands caressing her, and she could scarcely bear the wondrous agony that tore through her as he bent to take one hard swollen nipple between his lips.

Without haste he tormented her, without mercy he caressed her, between kisses removing their final few garments until at last they lay warm and naked together.

Leah pressed against him, dizzy from wanting him, her hands exploring with a sense of magical wonder every inch of his proud male body.

How could I have lived without him for all these years? How did I survive without him to love me?

Exultant with desire for him, she kissed him and caressed him. I was dead for all these years. The thought hammered inside her. I have been dead and now at last I have come alive again!

There were tears on her cheeks. She felt him kiss them. Then he was holding her firmly and sliding on top of her.

'*Sposa mia adorato...!*'

And then their bodies were one.

CHAPTER NINE

WHEN Leah came out of the bathroom, wrapped in a huge blue bathsheet, Vincenzo was sitting up in bed. At her frozen expression, the smile on his face faded.

'What's the matter?' he asked her. 'What have you been doing?'

Leah scarcely glanced at him. 'I was taking a shower.' With stiff, reproachful fingers she plucked her clothes from the floor, where they had been tossed an hour earlier in passionate abandon.

'Are you coming back to bed?' He flicked back the sheet beside him. 'Come on.' He smiled again. 'Leave your clothes where they are.'

'I'll do no such thing.' Grim-faced, she looked back at him, and her voice was shaky with emotion as she told him, 'I've just this minute finished cleansing myself of that regrettable lapse that took place between us. I don't intend sullying myself again.'

'Sullying yourself? Is that what you were doing?' All at once there was a distinct touch of razor in his tone. He threw back the bed sheet and swung his legs to the floor. 'It would appear then that the business of sullying yourself is something you rather enjoy.'

Leah kept her eyes averted as she hunted for her sandal. It was true, she had enjoyed it. Almost frighteningly. She could not deny that. But, almost immediately it was over, with a shock of horror she had come sharply to her senses.

'But you always were the great seducer, weren't you? The consummate lover! The all-round Romeo!' She threw the words at him like a condemnation. 'I suppose you're proud of behaving like a jungle cat!'

He rose to his feet slowly. 'I'm not the only jungle cat.' His voice was harsh. His eyes bored through her. 'I can assure you of that, my hot-blooded little leopardess.'

She had still not found her sandal and her nerves were stretched to breaking. Roughly, she pushed a chair aside and peered beneath it. How dared he have the gall to insult her when he was the one who was to blame for everything?

'I fear you're fooling yourself. What you mistook for passion was simply an expression of my absolute horror at the situation into which you had manipulated me!' As he simply smiled cynically at this effort to excuse herself, she shot him a look of vitriolic disapproval. 'Why don't you cover yourself? The party's over and I don't particularly enjoy having you standing there naked!'

More accurately, her anger was in danger of being dissipated by the splendid spectacle of his nudity. She turned her back on him as he ignored her protests and simply pointed out, his tone mocking and derisive,

'I'd say it's a little late for prudery. You had no objections to my naked body just a little while ago. In fact, I seem to remember you tearing my clothes off.'

'I did no such thing!' She had found the sandal. She snatched it up and turned to glare at him. 'More self-delusion, I'm afraid. You were the one who was tearing people's clothes off!' She tossed her head at him. 'But that's immaterial. All I was suggesting was that you behave with some decorum. We are, after all, both guests in Franca's home!'

'Ah, yes, so we are.' He smiled at her cynically, folding his arms across his broad chest. 'Aren't you ashamed to have seduced me beneath our dear hostess's roof?'

How could he make a joke of it? He was truly contemptible. 'You're the one who ought to be ashamed! Do you have no sense of propriety to make love to someone else in——'

She had been about to finish, In the home of your fiancée, but he cut in sharply, 'Not to "someone", to my wife. I see nothing whatsoever to be ashamed of in that.'

'No, you wouldn't!' Leah glared at him. 'You always did have the morals of an alleycat, so it's silly of me to be in the least surprised. Nothing about you changes, does it?'

'And nothing about you changes either, *sposa mia*. I suppose in the heat of the moment you forgot about Ronald?'

Leah felt herself flush. Yes, she had forgotten about Ronald. Ronald, her non-existent, make-believe fiancé. She turned away awkwardly. 'I'm going to my own room. Don't try to follow me. I have nothing more to say to you.'

'Oh, don't worry, I have no intention of following you. I've already had all I wanted from you, *cara*.'

His tone was biting, deliberately cruel. In spite of herself, Leah flinched beneath the lash of it. But she did not turn round and she did not answer him. On stiff legs she headed for the door.

But then he stopped her in her tracks. 'Oh, there's just one thing... Be good enough to inform me should you discover that you're pregnant.'

'Pregnant?' Leah's heart stopped. She turned round to look at him, aware that all the colour had drained from her face.

'It is possible, is it not? That is how these things happen. Or had you already taken precautions?'

'Precautions...no.' She shook her head numbly. The possibility that she might be pregnant frankly appalled her. That she might be taking such a risk had never entered her head.

She looked into his face, her stomach clenching with anger. It was his fault that she found herself faced with such a prospect. 'But please don't concern yourself about it,' she assured him, the words issuing like steel pellets from between her clenched teeth. 'If I am pregnant, I promise you you'll never know. I shall deal with it myself.'

'Deal? What do you mean, deal?' He had reached out to grab hold of her. His eyes burned black and merciless. 'Kindly explain.'

Leah tried to snatch her arm away, but he simply held her tighter. 'It's none of your damned business!' she spat at him furiously. '*I* know what I mean. I don't have to explain.'

'I'm afraid you do.' He shook her roughly. 'If there is a child, it is mine as well as yours.'

'Nothing of mine is yours!' she shot back at him with resentment. 'And if there is a child, you'll never be its father. Ronald would make a far better father than you!'

'So that's what you have in mind.' His tone had lost some of its harshness, but the grip of his fingers on her arm never slackened. 'You plan to bless this passionless marriage to Ronald with a ready-made baby that is partly mine?'

'If need be, yes.' She lied without a flicker. In reality, if there was a baby, she would bring it up alone. Then, truthfully, she added, 'As I already told you, I would make damned sure it was kept safely out of *your* clutches!'

He smiled darkly and released her. 'That might not be so easy. I do not part so easily with what is mine.' He stood over her, looking down at her. 'But this is all conjecture—and there will be time enough, should the need arise, for us to decide the fate of our child.'

Leah looked back at him, hating him. What had he lured her into? She had believed herself free of him and now, to her mounting horror, he seemed to be pressing in on her whichever way she turned.

She swung away from him shakily, clutching her bundle of clothing, and headed blindly for the door. And like some dark malevolent presence she could feel his eyes following her all the way along the corridor to the door of her own room.

It was pointless berating herself for what had happened. She'd made a horrible mistake and nothing could change that. Yet all night long, hour after endless hour, Leah couldn't stop thinking about how crazy she'd been.

Endlessly, she tried to analyse how it could have happened. Or, more accurately, how she could have *allowed* it to happen. How could she have allowed Vincenzo to make love to her?

It was the accident that was to blame. That almost-drowning, when he had come to her rescue and demolished her defences. All day she'd been uneasy, full of conflicting emotions, remembering past tenderness, false moments best forgotten, allowing herself to be seduced by his charms.

And how easily she had fallen. Just as she had five years ago, she'd thrown herself abandonedly into his faithless, cheating arms. Only it was worse this time. She'd had an excuse five years ago. She'd been desperately in love with him and had believed that he loved her. This time she had been under no such illusions. He had never loved her. And she no longer loved him.

Tears burned her eyes. So, why had she wanted him, so desperately, so overwhelmingly that she could not resist him? How come her flesh still burned at his touch in a way that it had burned for no other man? And why had making love with him been so sublime an experience that, while she was in his arms, she would have gladly sold her soul for him?

She closed her eyes tightly. And he had simply been using her, just as he had always used her.

Once the stakes had been higher, she thought with a shaft of bitterness. Five years ago he had used her in order to gain her father's company. This time, all he had been after was a fleeting moment of pleasure. She could have been anyone. It would have made no difference.

Long into the night she flayed and tormented herself. Then, finally, exhausted, she drifted into sleep.

The next couple of days were stiff and hostile. Barely a civil word passed between them.

For her part, Leah did her best to avoid him, keeping to her own little corner of the beach, eating her meals alone, spending long hours in her room. And though Vincenzo made no attempt to inflict his company on her, she could sense there was something eating into him. No doubt he was displeased by the way she had rejected him. Perhaps he had expected her to come running back for more.

Whatever the reason, he was looking for a confrontation, an opportunity to throw his weight around. She could tell by the way his eyes kept following her, dark and menacing, from room to room.

But she denied him the opportunity. She wanted nothing more to do with him, and besides she'd already had enough of his abuse. There was no way she intended to take any more.

It was only on his daily excursions to Paluro that Leah insisted on tagging along. And on every trip she prayed that they might be successful, that at last they'd have their chance to talk to Jo and Carlo, and that finally, mercifully, she would be free to fly home.

So far, alas, that had not happened. The 'lovebirds' had not returned to the villa.

They were headed there now, bombing along the *autostrada*, *Aida* booming at full blast from the speakers. Leah stared straight ahead, fingers crossed in her lap. Somehow, she had a feeling that today their luck might change.

As they came off the motorway and headed for the village, Leah felt herself tense in anticipation. Then, as they turned into the street where the villa stood, she held her breath and leaned forward to peer outside.

Then her heart leapt inside her. She turned to Vincenzo. 'Look! There's a car in the driveway! They must be here!'

He barely even glanced at her as he pulled on the handbrake. 'If they are, I warn you, let me handle this. I don't want you making things unnecessarily difficult.'

'You're the one who's likely to make them difficult!' She fumbled for the door-handle as he stepped out on to the pavement, totally ignoring her protest. Then she hurried after him as he strode towards the front door. 'Let me speak to Jo. Don't you dare try to bully her!'

His thumb was on the doorbell, imperious and impatient. 'Stay out of this, Leah. I've warned you already.'

'I won't stay out of it! Jo's my sister!' But she got no further, for suddenly the door opened.

Carlo was almost as tall as his uncle, but less well-muscled, more slenderly built. A strikingly handsome dark-haired boy, dressed in a T-shirt and faded jeans.

But, instantly, at the sight of Vincenzo, a dark scowl fell across his face.

'Che fai qui?' What are you doing here? he demanded belligerently. His gaze shifted, full of burning anger, to Leah, then back to his uncle. 'Why have you two come?'

Leah held her breath, expecting an explosion. Nobody spoke to Vincenzo like that. But to her astonishment she heard him reply in a calm voice, 'We've come to talk to you. May we come in?'

With unembellished reluctance, Carlo stood aside. 'I suppose I can't very well say no.' His tone was full of bubbling resentment. 'But I can promise you now that you're wasting your time.'

'That goes for you, too, Leah. I told you not to come.'

As Leah stepped into the villa behind Vincenzo, Jo suddenly appeared at the end of the hallway. Her normally lovely face was twisted with annoyance. 'Why didn't you do as I asked and just go home?'

Before Leah could respond, Vincenzo cut in, 'She didn't do as you asked because she happens to care for you. Just as I happen to care for my nephew.' He glanced again at Carlo. 'Neither of us wants you to make a terrible mistake.'

The four of them were standing awkwardly in the hall, Carlo now protectively at Jo's side, the two 'lovebirds' scowling at the intruders.

'Can we go and sit down?' Following Vincenzo's example, Leah kept her tone mild and reasonable. She smiled at her sister. 'Believe me, Jo, we haven't come here to lay down the law. We just want to talk to you, perhaps offer some advice.'

'We don't need your advice.' It was Carlo who responded. 'We don't need anyone's advice. We know what we're doing.'

'I'm sure you do.' Vincenzo's tone was still easy. Then he shrugged. 'Let's do as Leah suggested. Let's sit down and have a civilised chat.'

He was heading for the sitting-room as Jo responded tetchily, 'A civilised chat? Is that what you call it? What's civilised, I'd like to know, about you two poking your noses into what's none of your business?'

But even as she and Carlo continued to grumble, along with Leah, they were following him into the room, then seating themselves side by side on the sofa while Vincenzo and Leah took separate armchairs.

With a coolness that left Leah a little breathless—she had not believed him capable of such self-control—Vincenzo cast a quick glance round the room then let his gaze drift back to the lovers.

'I'd forgotten how lovely my sister's villa was. A perfect place for a romantic hideaway.' A smile touched his lips. 'I don't blame you in the slightest for taking the chance to enjoy each other's company here in private.'

The good-natured and patently sincere observation was met with surly, glowering silence. Leah felt a flicker of annoyance, but concealed it carefully as she proceeded to back up Vincenzo.

'We have nothing against your relationship,' she offered reasonably. It was not strictly true, though, as she said it, she realised it wasn't strictly untrue either. An innocent romance, even between a Blain and Petruzzi, as Vincenzo himself had said in the beginning, was hardly cause for deep concern.

She smiled and continued in the same reasonable tone, 'No one can tell another person who to fall in love with. All we're worried about is that you don't rush into anything. You're both very young and you haven't known each other long enough to be thinking of a serious commitment.'

As she said it, she let her eyes drift to Jo's left hand, relief flooding through her as she saw no sign of a ring there.

'Leah's right, there's plenty of time for that.' Vincenzo leaned forward in his chair. 'You, Jo, so Leah tells me, are due to start a course at university this autumn. It would be a big mistake to give that up, a mistake you might regret all your life.

'And Carlo...' he let his gaze shift back to his nephew '...Carlo is still carving out his career. He's in no position to take on the responsibilities of marriage. In a couple of years things will be different. If you still feel the same then, I won't try to stop you.'

'How decent of you!' Carlo snapped his response. 'Well, let me tell you something that may just surprise you! Not only will you not stop me doing what I want to in the future, you haven't a hope in hell of stopping me now! So, stop trying to interfere! What I do with my life is none of your damned business!'

Leah could feel the tension in Vincenzo tighten. He was like a big cat pushed too far and ready to spring. Instinctively, she reached out and laid a hand on his arm, as much to express her solidarity as to restrain him. Then in a clear voice, with just a hint of pleading, she addressed herself to Jo and Carlo.

'Of course it's your life and maybe it is none of our business. But the only reason we're here is because we care for you——'

'You said that already, but your concern doesn't interest us.' Taking Jo with him, Carlo snapped to his feet. 'We really don't want to listen to any more of this!'

'Jo, *please* listen...' There was a sob in Leah's voice. 'Not so long ago I was in your same position and I made the biggest mistake of my life.' As she started to stand up, her legs felt shaky. 'I don't want you to make the same mistake I made. I don't want you to be destroyed as I was.'

But Jo just shook her head. 'That was your life. This is mine. So kindly just do as Carlo said and stay out of it. I don't want your advice.'

The next moment the two of them were running from the room, heading down the hallway towards the front door. As Leah started to hurry after them, Vincenzo caught her arm gently. 'Let them go. It's useless,' he said.

She knew he was right, but she pulled herself free and went rushing to the door just in time to see Carlo's car speed off into the road. And suddenly she felt like weeping. After all their efforts, they had failed.

Leah did not hear Vincenzo come to stand beside her. The first thing she was aware of was his hand on her waist. Then she heard him say softly, 'Was that true what you said? About being destroyed by what happened between us?'

'Yes, it was true.' She shifted away from him. Suddenly her eyes ached with unshed tears. 'You ruined my life. You tore me to pieces. You'll never know how close I came to falling apart.'

She had said too much. She turned away abruptly, took a deep breath and changed the subject. 'Jo may think this is over, but it isn't. I won't let her make the same mistake I made.'

'And what was your mistake?'

'Marrying you.'

'Why?'

'Because you never loved me.'

'Didn't I?'

'No. All you ever did was use me.'

It hurt to say it and to see his calm reaction. He shrugged. 'And what makes you so sure that's true?'

'Oh, I'm sure all right.' Her heart was beating painfully, as it always did when she thought of these things. 'I heard. I saw. I understood.' She turned away abruptly. 'I had plenty of proof.'

He did not try to stop her as she headed for the car. She heard the front door close, then his footsteps follow her down the drive. And as he climbed into the car beside her, he asked her no more questions. In fact, he did not say a word.

But as they headed out of Paluro and back to the motorway, Leah was filled with a weight of deep foreboding. She sensed this conversation was far from over. And perhaps, she thought with an ache of resentment, it was time to confront him with what she knew.

CHAPTER TEN

NEITHER of them spoke a word on the journey back to the villa.

Leah was still seething with emotion—and her turmoil, if she was honest, had little to do with Jo. It was the man at her side, composed and silent, who had set off this maelstrom in her heart. The memory of past hurts she had believed long forgotten, resentments and bitterness she had buried long ago. *He* had awakened them to torment and torture her. It was he who was ensuring they would never let her go.

She slid a brief look at the implacable dark profile. Over the past couple of days she had sensed quite sharply that Vincenzo was in the mood for a confrontation. But she had been ultra-careful to give him no opening. A confrontation was something she'd preferred to avoid.

But now, quite suddenly, her mood had altered. That sense of foreboding she'd felt back at Paluro had transformed itself with every passing kilometre into something much more bold and positive.

Let him have his confrontation. And let him have it immediately. He would discover she knew more of the truth than he realised. She would reveal him for the liar and the fraud that he was. Let him try to claim then that he had not ruined her life!

And perhaps then, she thought desperately, once it was all out in the open, she would finally be free of him, her secrets all off-loaded, no more hidden rancour, her soul scoured clean. Perhaps then she could finally turn her back on him, at peace, as though he had never been.

They drew up outside the villa with a spluttering of tyres, and, still without a word or a glance in her direction, Vincenzo opened the driver's door and quickly climbed out.

As he headed for the front door, Leah hurried after him. 'I think you and I should have a talk.'

'Another one?' He smiled a harsh, sardonic smile. 'What makes you think we have anything to talk about?'

'I think we do.' Her gaze did not flicker. 'And I happen to believe that you think so, too.'

'And since when did you know what I thought about anything? Eh, *sposa mia*? Answer me that?'

Leah pursed her lips. He was being deliberately obstructive. But then she ought to have expected that. She took a deep breath. 'Well, *I* want to talk to you. And, if it's all the same, I want to talk now.'

He had pushed the front door open and was stepping into the hallway. 'I'm afraid, *sposa mia*, it's not all the same.' His tone was biting. He did not look at her. 'Right now the only talk I intend having is with the seagulls.' He tossed the front door key on to a carved gilt table. 'If you have no objections, I'm going for a swim.'

Damn him to oblivion! Totally powerless to stop him, Leah stood and watched as he strode across the hall and down the narrow passageway that led to the back of the house. How he loved to torment her, to play his games and see her suffer. How he loved to be in control!

Well, I can wait! Biting back her frustration, Leah headed for the drawing-room and poured herself a soda-water. Then she seated herself stiffly in the sofa by the window with its panoramic view out over the beach and the sea.

It was perhaps not the best seat she could have chosen. As she raised her glass to take a sip of her drink, Vincenzo suddenly came into view.

He was pulling off his shoes, shedding his socks, then dumping his shirt and trousers on the sand. She tried to look away, to still the fluttering inside her, but her eyes were still on him as he stepped out of his shorts to stand powerful and naked at the water's edge.

Her breath caught in her throat. He was so damned beautiful. So exciting, so desirable. To see him made her heart ache.

With a gasp of impatience she rose to her feet and took another quick gulp of her drink. He was none of these things. She was fooling herself. He was the devil in disguise and she was an idiot.

She saw him dive into the water and strike out towards the horizon, a vivid streak of crimson as sunset approached. And for a moment she stood mesmerised to watch his progress—the powerful arms that cut through the water like knives, the dark head moving rhythmically from side to side.

If only, she thought, he would keep on swimming forever and never come anywhere near her again.

It was half an hour later when he walked into the drawing-room, evidently surprised to find her there.

'Still here, I see.' His tone was hostile. 'I was really rather hoping you might have gone to your room.'

'Sorry to disappoint you.' Her heart was suddenly racing. 'But I did say earlier that I wanted to talk to you.'

'Ah, yes, of course.' His tone was mocking, as he crossed to the drinks table and poured a small whisky. 'However, when you say "talk"——' he smiled cynically over his shoulder '—I take it a scene is what you really have in mind?'

'Not exactly.' She smiled cynically back at him. 'Though, no doubt, a scene is what you'll turn it into.'

'What *I'll* turn it into? I seem to recall that *you* were the one with a taste for hysterical little scenes.'

'Changed days.' Leah took a mouthful of her soda-water. 'You are no longer capable of stirring up such passions in me.'

'No?'

'No.' She took another quick mouthful of her drink to drown the faint stir of emotion inside her. Then she looked him in the eye. 'You no longer have that power, which is probably a blessing for both of us.'

As he simply smiled and took a mouthful of his whisky, then came to seat himself in one of the armchairs opposite her, Leah could feel the tension in her easing slightly. She was beginning to feel pleasantly in control.

He leaned back against the cushions of the armchair. 'So, what was it you wanted to talk about?'

Her heart skipped a half-beat. She needed a moment more, a fraction more time to collect herself fully before embarking on the emotionally charged subject before her. And, besides, there was another small matter to clear up first.

She glanced down into her soda-water. 'About Jo and Carlo... What do you think our next move should be?'

'Jo and Carlo? That's what you want to talk about?'

'For the moment. So, what's your answer?'

He sat back in his seat, adjusting the cushion at his shoulders. 'I haven't decided yet what I'm going to do next.'

'But you are going to do something? You're not just going to leave it? I mean, nothing has changed. We still have to try and stop them.'

'*We?* I don't think I much care for that pronoun. If either of us is going to do anything, I suggest it's alone.'

'But I don't know where they are!'

'Neither do I.'

'Maybe, but you have a better chance of tracking them down than I do. You know people here. You have contacts. You can speak to Carlo's friends. I don't even know who his friends are!'

'That's right, you don't. That puts you at a disadvantage. If I were you, I'd give up and go home.'

So, they were right back at the beginning again, where they had been in Rome. With a gasp of impatience Leah jumped to her feet, crossed to the drinks table and poured herself more soda.

But as she swung back towards the sofa the toe of her sandal caught in a corner of the rug and she stumbled awkwardly, very nearly falling.

'Sober as a judge, I see.' Vincenzo's tone was scathing, as with a gasp of annoyance she regained her equilibrium and reseated herself once more on the sofa.

'I am sober, actually.' Leah bit the words across at him. 'Soda-water is all I've been drinking.'

But he was scarcely listening to her as his dark eyes bit into her. 'This whole little scene is becoming all too familiar. Any minute now, if my memory serves me, we'll be subjected to a display of tears and tantrums. Perhaps even a bit of wilful destruction. However...' He paused. 'I must ask you to control yourself. This time it won't be my house you're destroying. Remember, you're a guest of Franca's.'

Leah pinned him with a look. 'I think you're exaggerating slightly. Breaking a couple of plates scarcely ranks as destroying a house.'

'They were very rare plates. Irreplaceable. And if I hadn't taken measures to stop you, who knows what other damage you might have done?'

What he was saying was humiliating. Leah hated him for it. The episodes he was referring to were something she was ashamed of. And besides, he knew full well that it was he who had provoked them.

She gripped her glass tightly. 'I know what you're referring to.' She narrowed her eyes in angry challenge. 'But so what if I got drunk a couple of times during the period I had the misfortune to be married to you? Are you really so surprised? You drove me to it!'

He smiled dismissively. 'Oh, it was always my fault. Whenever you acted badly, I was to blame.'

'Yes, you were!' Resentment burned through her. How dared he make a mockery of the truth? 'I was unhappy. Desperately unhappy. Nineteen years old and married to a man who always had better things to do than spend time with me. Who could really blame me if I consoled myself with a drink or two?'

'The man you were married to was out making a living! He happened to be at a crucial point in his career!'

'You expect me to believe that? I didn't then and I still don't. You were out at nightclubs entertaining your girlfriends!' Angrily, she continued, 'And don't accuse me of being a drunk! I know I made a ridiculous fool of myself, but it only happened on a couple of occasions!'

'Oh, don't worry, I haven't forgotten. They were memorable occasions. No one could forget a spectacle like that.'

Leah glanced down at her glass, fighting to control her sudden trembling. She, too, was never likely to forget, though she had sought for five years to banish the memory.

It had been another Leah then, a poor wretched child, distraught with misery, racked with pain at the evidence that her marriage was no more than a sham. At first she had tried to hide what was happening to her, the slow disintegration of her soul, the agony that was tearing her poor heart to pieces.

That first time, she remembered, she had stayed up to confront him, to demand that he finally confess his infidelity. She had taken the first drink for courage, and then another, and by the time he had come home she'd been out of her senses.

She remembered only dimly the hysteria that had possessed her, how she'd screamed and accused and wept and pleaded—and reaped for her pains only his anger and derision.

The second time had been worse. That was when she'd flung the plates at him, missing him by a mile, scarcely able to stand upright.

And that was when she'd known that she had to leave him. To have stayed would have meant her eventual destruction. And she could not risk that. Things were bad enough already. She had lost control, and her pride along with it.

She glanced up at him now and narrowed her eyes. 'I wanted to go then, to let you get on with your life without me. Since you despised me so much, why didn't you just let me?'

'Because you were my wife.' He looked back at her steadily. 'For better or for worse you belonged with me.'

'Ah, yes...*belonged*... That's the operative word. I belonged to you, like some possession. That's why you wouldn't let me go.' Hadn't she always known that he held on as tight as a clam to anything that was his?

'But you always knew that. I told you right from the beginning. And I also told you there was only one thing in the world that would ever induce me to let you go.'

Leah felt her cheeks flush and drain simultaneously. Yes, he had told her, and that knowledge was what had saved her. For he had warned her that only in the event of her infidelity would he ever be prepared to release her.

He looked into her face now. 'You know, you surprised me. Even disappointed me a little. If you had to be unfaithful, you might at least have chosen someone a little better.'

Leah threw him a scathing look. 'Did you find it demeaning that I should prefer the embraces of some unpretentious car mechanic to those of my rich and powerful husband? Perhaps you would have preferred it if I'd been cheating with the bank manager?'

Vincenzo smiled without humour and did not answer immediately. His dark eyes seemed to scrutinise her face. He took a mouthful of his drink. 'As a matter of fact, no. I would not have preferred that any better. There's many a car mechanic I esteem more than some bank managers, but this particular car mechanic, as you yourself must have been aware, had something of a reputation. He'd slept with every available woman in the district. Plus a few,' he added wryly, 'who were not available.'

'So people said.' Leah met his gaze with difficulty. The hand around her glass all at once felt clammy. 'Personally, I wasn't interested in his reputation.'

'Evidently not.' His gaze did not flicker. 'And that was what surprised me a little. For all your faults, I would have expected you to be a little more discriminating.'

'Like when I married you, you mean?' She snatched the opportunity to change the subject. 'I showed a great deal of discrimination when I married you, didn't I?' Her tone was sarcastic. 'And look where it got me!'

He shook his head. 'Indeed,' he observed. Then he took another mouthful of his drink. 'Another thing that surprised me with that affair was your honesty. I would never have suspected if you hadn't told me.'

Leah gripped her glass tightly as her heart skipped a beat. But almost instantly she regained her composure. 'No, I suppose you wouldn't. You're so damned vain it would never occur to you for a moment to suspect that your wife might prefer another man.'

'Why did you tell me?'

'I wanted to hurt you. I wanted to hurt you as you kept on hurting me.'

'But he'd already left you. The affair was over. He'd already moved north to Milan.'

'That didn't change anything. What had happened had happened. And I was glad it had happened and I wanted you to know.'

Vincenzo contemplated his glass in silence. 'Had there been others or was he really the only one?'

'If there had been others, don't worry, I would have told you. That would have been my pleasure. I wouldn't have kept it a secret.' She took a deep breath and once more sought to change the subject. 'You, remember, were the one with all the secrets. You were the one who kept your affairs hidden.'

He regarded her candidly. 'What affairs?' he queried. 'I'd be most grateful if you'd finally enlighten me.'

Leah laughed at that. 'Why bother to keep on lying? It's all ancient history and, after all, we're to be divorced soon.'

'Indeed we are. But, I assure you, I'm not lying. I was never unfaithful to you, *sposa mia*.'

His insistence was irritating. Leah *knew* he was lying. 'You seriously expect me to believe that all those evenings you told me you were out entertaining clients that really was what you were doing?'

He shook his head. 'No, I don't expect you to believe it, but nevertheless it happens to be true. Even if I'd wanted to, at that point in my career, there was no way I could have fitted in an affair, let alone the string of them that you accused me of. I was working sixteen hours a day.'

A self-mocking smile flitted across his features, as he drained his glass and laid it to one side. 'Even a man of my legendary stamina only has so much energy to spread around. I'd never have made it to my thirtieth birthday if even half of what you accused me of was true!'

He was a persuasive liar. But still Leah shook her head. Her disbelief was too deeply ingrained to be swept away by such whimsical arguments.

'Besides,' he continued, 'why would I be unfaithful? I was newly married to a beautiful young girl whom I believed to be deeply in love with me.'

That much was true. Her love had been infinite. 'In love, but inexperienced.' Leah's tone was bitter. 'Perhaps you preferred more experienced women?'

Vincenzo smiled. 'You were gaining experience. With each night that passed you were becoming a better lover. You had a natural flair. You had passion. You had enthusiasm.' He held her gaze a moment. 'You still have, *sposa mia*.'

At his words a sweet longing pierced her loins like a bayonet. She glanced away quickly, annoyed at herself. Then she raised her eyes again and accused him softly, 'But you still had good reason for being unfaithful.'

He frowned across at her. 'What reason did I have?'

'I told you already. You never loved me. That's a good enough reason, as I see it. Why should you be faithful to a wife you didn't love?'

His eyes flickered with impatience, but he offered no denial. 'Why do you insist on believing that I never loved you? Why on earth would I have married you if I didn't?'

That was precisely the question she'd been waiting for. Leah felt her stomach clench tightly inside her. She laid down her glass and looked across at him. 'Don't worry, I can answer that one easily. You married me to get your hands on Blain Cars.'

She'd never said it before. Shame had kept her silent. When she'd discovered that it was so she'd felt like a piece of merchandise.

'I *what*?' For a moment Vincenzo blinked at her. One might genuinely have believed he was taken aback. 'What on earth gave you that idea?' he demanded.

'Oh, don't play the innocent! You wanted the company badly. You would have done anything to get your hands on it!'

'I don't deny I wanted it badly. That was why I was prepared to pay your father top price.'

'And why you thought it was worth the sacrifice of marrying me!'

'What sacrifice? What the hell are you talking about? Your father was going to sell me the company anyway. I didn't have to make any damned sacrifice!'

'You couldn't be sure! He had a few good offers. And you know as well as I do that he sold it to you to keep it in the family, when you proposed to me!'

He was staring across at her as though she'd gone crazy. 'I don't believe this!' He jumped to his feet. 'You seriously believe that I married you simply in order to get my hands on your father's company?'

'Oh, I didn't believe it at the time. I believed your lies. I was fooled by your charm. Just as both of my parents were. But I soon found out what an idiot I'd been. Once it was too late, I discovered the truth.'

'What truth? What did you discover?' He was pacing the floor. He came to stand before her, his dark eyes blazing. 'Come on! Out with it! What did you discover?'

Leah's heart was beating frantically inside her, just as it always did when she cast her mind back to that summer's evening at the Villa Petruzzi when, alone in the drawing-room, she'd overheard the truth. But this time she made no effort to suppress her feelings, for all that was precisely what she'd been planning to tell him. The story that she hoped that, once out in the open, would purge him from her soul for ever.

'I'll tell you,' she assured him, struggling for composure. She moistened her lips. Her mouth had gone dry.

'Well, I'm waiting!' Vincenzo was impatient. 'Are you going to tell me what you're talking about or not?'

His impatience provided her with the focus she needed. Her nervousness vanished to be replaced by cool anger. 'As soon as you stop shouting at me, I'll tell you. Why don't you sit down? I can't bear you standing over me!'

He did not sit down, but he turned away abruptly, snatching his empty glass up from the table, and crossed to pour himself another drink.

'I'm listening,' he growled at her over his shoulder. 'Kindly do me a favour and get on with it.'

Leah sat back in her seat and took a deep breath. Suddenly she wasn't quite sure where to start.

'We were in Rome, at the villa...' She might as well start at the beginning. 'Your friend Piero and his wife were spending the weekend with us.'

'Piero and Maria?'

'Yes, Piero and Maria. We were all getting ready to go out for the evening. Maria was upstairs and presumably you thought I was, too, when you and Piero came in from the garden and stood chatting for a couple of minutes in the hall...'

'But you weren't in the bedroom?' He had turned round to face her.

'No, I was in the drawing-room and the door was half open. I could hear every word you said.'

He was still by the drinks table. 'And what did you hear?' His eyes were narrowed, his expression inscrutable.

'I heard...' Her heart was thumping. Again, she licked her lips. 'I heard Piero say to you—and I happen to remember the words precisely... I heard him say, "You know, you're a lucky devil. I reckon, after all, that was a pretty good deal you made. A useful little English company and a pretty little English bride. I don't know why you were complaining so much about losing your freedom. For a deal like that it's not much of a sacrifice."'

'And what did I say?' As she paused for breath, he remained standing where he was, his glass in his hand, that same unreadable look on his face.

Leah sighed. 'You said, "You're probably right. And, besides, I don't intend to let it cramp my style."'

There was a silence as she came to the end of her story. Heart beating, she stared down into her lap. Even now the memory could pulverise her soul.

He had taken a step towards her. 'That's it?' he was asking. 'That's the sum total of what you overheard?'

Her eyes snapped up, dark with resentment. 'Yes, that's all! Wouldn't you say it was enough?'

'I would say that if that's what's been eating into you, convincing you for all these years that I didn't love you, that I only married you for your father's company, it's time you realised that you understood nothing.' He frowned and took another step towards her. 'Piero wasn't saying what you thought he was saying. I'm afraid you got hold of the wrong end of the stick.'

The wrong end of the stick! A likely story! Suddenly angry at his gall, Leah jumped to her feet to face him. 'I suppose you have a nice convenient explanation as to how I could possibly have managed to do that?'

'As a matter of fact, I have.'

'Well, I don't want to hear it! I don't want to hear any more of your lies!'

'I'm sorry, but you're going to listen to me anyway.' He was reaching out towards her. 'I'm afraid I insist.'

Leah tried to dart away from him, but he would have caught her, except for the fact that in that very same instant Franca came hurrying into the room.

She was flushed and breathless. 'Thank heavens you're here!' With only a quick glance at Leah, she beckoned to Vincenzo. 'Please come at once. I've got a problem. My car broke down and I had to get a taxi and I haven't got a penny in my purse to pay the driver. And besides, I'm sure he's over-charging me. I need you to come and deal with him for me. He's making such a terrible fuss!'

Leah saw Vincenzo hesitate. He scowled with annoyance. Then he looked straight into her eyes. 'Don't move from this room. As soon as I come back, we'll resume this conversation.' Then reluctantly he turned on his heel and followed Franca out into the hall.

Leah wasted not a moment. She snatched up her bag. Then, running as though her feet were on fire, she flew from the room and along the passage that led to the back door of the house.

Breathlessly, a moment later she was heading along the pathway that ran behind the house, between the rear garden and the beach. Then she was plunging between the trees that bordered the road, emerging almost in the same split second that the taxi which had brought Franca home suddenly appeared round the bend.

She waved it down and collapsed inside.

'Take me to the nearest railway station,' she ordered the driver. 'I have to catch a train to Rome.'

CHAPTER ELEVEN

IT WAS a crazy impulse that had caused her to fly off like that. Self-defence, Leah told herself wryly. It had been hard enough admitting to that humiliating revelation—whenever she thought of it her blood turned to ice-water—without also having to listen to Vincenzo's tawdry excuses. To endure that would only have humiliated her even more.

Besides, she realised, she needed to get away from him. With each day that passed she was losing control of her emotions—to the extent that, at times, in a way that scared her, she scarcely even knew what her emotions were.

Of course, she still hated him. She would never stop hating him, though she could scarcely deny that she still found him physically attractive. That had been made all too painfully clear. But what disconcerted her were those unexpected moments of tenderness, moments when she would look at him and feel a warm rush inside her, just as she'd used to in the early days of their marriage. In those days when, like the sun, he had been the light of her world.

Such feelings confused her, even scared her a little. She found them impossible to rationalise away. Tenderness had no place in her feelings for Vincenzo. It was a dangerous madness. A betrayal of herself.

The sooner I get away from Italy, the better, she told herself as she checked back into her Rome hotel. Once I'm back in London, that will be the end of all this madness. Soon the divorce will be through and then I'll be free. Free never to think of him again.

But there was still the problem of Jo to be resolved. Yet where to begin when she hadn't a clue where her sister and Carlo might have gone? Without much hope, she phoned the rented Rome apartment, but, as she had expected, there was no reply.

Perhaps, she thought unhappily, she should have stayed around Paluro and tried quizzing their neighbours as to where they might have gone. One thing was for certain, they would not have gone back to the villa. But that was the only thing she could be sure of.

In a dejected frame of mind, after a half-eaten dinner, she was getting ready for bed when the telephone rang.

With a flicker of trepidation Leah lifted the receiver. Pray God it wasn't Vincenzo on the other end.

But to her astonishment and delight it was Jo who spoke to her, 'Leah, it's me. Are you all right?' She sounded breathless and a little worried.

'Of course I'm all right—but how about you? Where are you, Jo? Is something wrong?'

'Nothing's wrong. We're on our way back to Rome. I want to come and talk to you.'

As Leah smiled with relief, Jo added quickly, 'Look, I can't talk now. I'm on a public phone and my money's running out. I'll come straight to your hotel as soon as I arrive. Promise me that you'll wait up?'

'Of course I'll wait up. I can't wait to see you.'

'OK. I'm off now. See you later.'

Leah had been about to ask, 'How long will you be?' but in that very instant the phone went dead. As she laid down the receiver, she glanced at her watch. It was just gone ten, reasonably early. Depending on where her sister had been phoning from she could be tapping on her door in half an hour's time or she might not arrive till after midnight.

Either way, it didn't matter, Leah thought to herself, smiling, as she pulled off her nightdress and pulled on a loose shift. She would wait up until the wee small hours, if necessary! She was just so relieved that Jo had got in touch.

She poured herself an orange juice from the fridge-bar, switched on the TV and sat down on the bed. But she wasn't paying attention to what was on the screen. Instead, she was rehearsing in her head what she would say to Jo when she finally appeared.

This time she would *make* her listen, if she had to tie her to one of the chairs! But perhaps, she mused, with a flicker of optimism, her sister was in the mood for listening anyway. Why else, after all, would she be coming to see her?

Leah sipped her drink and flicked through the channels. If everything went well, if she managed to convince Jo that rushing into marriage would be a fatal mistake, then she could book her flight home tomorrow morning and put this whole disastrous episode behind her.

The more she considered it, the more the prospect warmed her. Soon she would be back in control of her life.

She leaned back against the pillows. What a wonderful prospect! And never again, as long as she lived, would she ever set foot in Rome, she vowed.

It was just gone quarter to eleven when she heard footsteps coming down the corridor. She switched off the TV and sat up straight, listening. Then, to her absolute delight, there was a knock on the door.

Leah leapt to her feet. 'I'm coming!' she called. Then, beaming a welcome, she pulled open the door. But at the sight that met her eyes, her heart shrivelled inside her.

'What are you doing here?' Her smile had vanished.

There was no hint of a smile on Vincenzo's face, either. 'I brought you this.' With dark narrowed eyes, he held out the weekend bag she had left behind at Franca's.

Leah snatched it from him. 'Thank you. You can go now. You shouldn't have come here. I have nothing to say to you.'

'Ah, but I have plenty to say to you.' Before she could close the door on him, Vincenzo had caught firm hold of the handle, and was pushing the door wide, then stepping briskly past her. 'In fact,' he enlarged, his tone impatient, 'I have several things I want to say to you.'

'But I don't want to hear them.' Leah was fuming. She stood immobile by the still open door, her features pale and tight with anger. 'And, what's more, I don't want you here in my room.' She dropped the bag on the floor and gestured with her thumb. 'So, kindly be good enough to leave immediately.'

She might as well have addressed herself to the furniture. With a gesture of pure arrogance, looking her straight in the eye, Vincenzo seated himself in

one of the armchairs, unbuttoning his linen jacket
and making himself comfortable.

'I shall leave when I've finished saying what I
came here to tell you.' He stretched out his legs.
'And not a moment before.'

'I want you to leave now. In fact, I insist.' Brist-
ling, Leah continued to stand by the open door.

'I don't care what you want.' He laid his hands
along the chair arms. 'So, insist all you like. I
promise you it'll get you nowhere.' He paused and
crossed his long legs at the ankles. 'So, you really
may as well close the door. Unless you want
everyone to overhear our business.'

Leah glared at him impotently. If she'd had the
strength, she would have lifted him bodily from the
chair and ejected him. She toyed briefly with the
idea of telling him she was expecting Jo, wondering
if that might persuade him to leave. But, knowing
him, that would merely encourage him to stay, so
she abandoned the idea and put up a silent prayer
that he would have finished what he'd come for
before Jo appeared.

Reluctantly, with a firm click, she closed the
door. Then she walked halfway across the floor
towards him and folded her arms across her chest.

'I hope you haven't come here to offer some cock
and bull excuse for that conversation with Piero
that I told you I overheard...?' She paused,
knowing in her heart that that was precisely why
he'd come. Her eyes gleamed impatiently. 'You'd
be wasting your time.'

'Would I? We'll see.' Vincenzo raised one dark
eyebrow, then narrowed his eyes at her and in an
angry tone accused her, 'That was a damned idiotic
thing you did, rushing off like that, without a word

to anyone. We searched all over for you. I even took a boat out, just in case you'd gone swimming and had got into trouble. Damn it!' His fist came down impatiently on the chair arm. 'Can't you ever behave in a responsible fashion?'

It had never occurred to her that he and Franca might be worried. Foolishly, she had assumed that they would guess what had happened. She felt a stab of guilt—mingled with a surprising flicker of gladness. Had he really gone to so much trouble? Had he genuinely cared that something might have happened to her?

Annoyed at herself, she pushed the thought away as he continued, 'Fortunately, before we got round to phoning the police, the solution to the mystery suddenly occurred to me. I phoned the cab company and they confirmed that one of their cabs had picked you up and taken you to the station.' He added unnecessarily, 'I was bloody furious. Don't you ever think of how your actions might affect others?'

He had a right to be angry. Leah realised that. But she was in no mood at all to be apologetic towards him.

She regarded him defiantly. 'That's good coming from you. When did you ever give a thought for other people?'

With a sigh of resignation, Vincenzo shook his head. 'How predictable you are, *sposa mia*. According to you, you're irreproachable. I'm the one who's guilty of all the sins in the universe.'

'And a few more besides. I'm glad you realise it.'

He ignored her gibe. 'How does it feel to be perfect? It must be nice to know that your every single action, however base and selfish it might appear to others, is nevertheless absolutely and totally justified.' He smiled a mocking smile. 'You must have one foot in heaven.'

At that moment Leah felt as though she had two feet in hell. Even without the added aggravation of his conversation, just his presence in the room with her was making her head spin. Her heart was beating strangely. Her limbs felt oddly leaden. The effects of her suppressed fury, she assured herself firmly.

She made an effort to throw off these unfortunate symptoms, took a deep breath and folded her arms more firmly. 'If you've come here to reprimand me because I left without telling you, then you've made your point. You can go now.'

'And another thing.' He frowned at her, ignoring her suggestion. 'Isn't it your custom to thank your hostess for her hospitality? Don't you think it was a little ill-mannered just to leave as you did?'

Leah sighed impatiently. 'I'll write her a note immediately. I'm extremely sorry that I forgot my manners.' She paused. 'Does that satisfy you? Now will you leave?'

'Not just yet.' He leaned back more comfortably. 'Why don't you sit down? Relax a little.'

She would relax once he'd gone and not a moment before. Through narrowed eyes Leah glared down into his face. 'Kindly get on with what you've come for. I'm rather tired. I'd like to get to bed.'

'All the more reason to sit down, don't you think?' He was being deliberately infuriating. 'You'd be much more comfortable.'

'I don't need to be comfortable to hear what you're saying. Besides, I rather enjoy looking down on you.'

Vincenzo smiled at that. 'Suit yourself, *sposa mia.*' Then he seemed to scrutinise her face for a moment. 'Why did you go rushing off like that?'

'I would have thought that was obvious. To get away from you. I find your company distasteful in the extreme.'

The insult slid over him. 'To get away from me ... or to avoid having to hear what I was about to tell you?' The dark eyes narrowed. 'Why were you afraid to listen?'

'Afraid? I wasn't afraid!' She dropped her arms to her sides now and stuffed her hands into the pockets of her shift. 'Why should I be afraid of anything you have to say to me? What an absolutely ridiculous idea!'

'I think perhaps it is not so ridiculous.' He regarded her with eyes that seemed to see inside her head. 'What I have to tell you could turn your judgement of me—and of our marriage—upside-down.'

Leah looked back at him. 'What you have to tell me will be a lie. And that's why I didn't want to hear it. I've already heard enough of your lies to last me for a dozen lifetimes.'

Vincenzo sighed impatiently. 'Try listening first.' Then he sat up abruptly, making her heart jump. 'And for heaven's sake, stop hovering about there! Sit down and stop acting like a child!'

To her own mild astonishment, Leah found herself obeying. Because I'm tired of standing and not because he told me to, she assured herself, as she sat down a little stiffly on the edge of the chair opposite him.

She crossed her legs at the ankles and laid her hands in her lap. 'OK, I'm listening. Get on with it,' she challenged him.

To her sharp dismay, he moved his own chair closer, so that they were only inches apart. He leaned towards her. 'I want you to listen carefully.' His eyes, as he spoke, were earnest and unblinking. 'It's important that you understand what I'm about to say.'

Important to whom? Leah wondered, looking back at him, the question reflected in the cynical glint in her eyes. Certainly, to her it was of minimal importance that she should understand the full complex content of the fable he was about to spin her.

But she said nothing, just nodded and waited for him to begin. The sooner he got started, the sooner he would be finished. Then her ordeal would be over and she would demand that he leave.

His elbows were on his thighs, his body bent forward, his hands clasped loosely between his knees. He said, 'If I remember rightly, what you heard Piero saying was more or less this: "I reckon, after all, that was a pretty good deal you made. A useful little English company and a pretty little English bride. I don't know why you were complaining so much about losing your freedom. For a deal like that it's not much of a sacrifice."'

He paused, one eyebrow lifting. 'Is that correct?'

In spite of herself, Leah was mildly impressed. His powers of recall were pretty formidable.

She nodded. 'That's correct. That's what I heard.'

'And my reply was: "You're probably right. And, besides, I don't intend to let it cramp my style"?'

Again, he had remembered what she had told him, verbatim. 'That's exactly what you said. I'll never forget it.' And to recall it still sent a dagger through her heart. Her gaze flickered away for just a moment, then she forced herself to look into his face again. How on earth did he hope to talk his way out of that?

He took a deep breath. 'I wish you'd mentioned this to me years ago. The whole thing's a total misunderstanding on your part. Piero and I weren't saying what you thought we were saying.'

'It sounded plain enough to me.' Her tone was brittle. 'I really don't think there was any misunderstanding.'

'Ah, but there was.' He sat back a little. 'When you heard Piero say: "I don't know why you were complaining about losing your freedom. For a deal like that it's not much of a sacrifice..." you thought that what he was referring to was our marriage; that I'd been complaining about sacrificing my freedom as a bachelor and that the only reason I'd done it was to swing the deal with your father...?'

As he paused, Leah nodded. 'It was quite plain, as I said.'

'But you're wrong. I wasn't talking about our marriage. The freedom I was complaining about losing had nothing at all to do with you.'

Leah continued to watch him, holding her breath. Through her disbelief, suddenly she felt anxious.

Vincenzo sighed. 'Before you overheard us, I recall that Piero and I had been out in the garden, discussing some of the legalities of my takeover of Blain Cars. One of the things that I'd been com-

plaining about were the various small restrictions
that your Department of Trade and Industry were
likely to impose on me as an overseas owner. I was
afraid I might not be as free as I am in Italy to run
things in the style that I'm accustomed to.

'That was what I meant by cramping my style.
Not even obliquely was I referring to our marriage.'

As he paused, there was a silence as deafening
as thunder. Wordlessly, Leah shook her head. It
simply was not possible that what she had believed
for all these years—the belief which had sounded
the death-knell of her marriage—was, as he had
told her, a mere tragic misunderstanding.

She pushed that terrible possibility from her and
answered him in a voice that was not quite steady.
'That's a very glib and clever explanation. But I'm
afraid I don't believe a single word of it.' She took
a deep breath. 'You *were* talking about me. Just a
moment before he spoke about you and your lost
freedom, Piero was saying that you'd made a good
deal—a useful little English company and a pretty
little English bride.' Through barely focused eyes
she glared across at him. 'Don't try to tell me that
I imagined *that*!'

'You didn't imagine any of it. What you did,
sposa mia, was put two and two together and make
five instead of four.' He shook his head. 'That
comment of Piero's was perhaps not in the best of
taste. Men sometimes make that sort of comment
to one another when they believe they're not being
overheard.'

He leaned towards her suddenly. 'But you must
believe me: my marriage to you and my deal with
your father were two totally and utterly separate
things.' He smiled a strange smile. 'Surely, you

couldn't believe that even I could be capable of such a cynical act?'

But she *had* believed it, and that belief had changed her life. She stared back at him now in blind horror and confusion. Was it really possible that she'd made a ghastly mistake?

He was frowning as he continued, 'I married you because I loved you. Surely you knew that? How could you have doubted it? The way I felt about you was perfectly plain.'

The only thing that had been perfectly plain had been her own almost obsessional fear of losing him. How could an unworldly nineteen-year-old like her satisfy a man like him?

She peered across at him now. 'But what about those other women? All those evenings you left me at the villa on my own. You wouldn't have done that if you'd really loved me.'

'But there were no other women! I've told you that endlessly.' He had reached across suddenly and taken hold of her hands. 'I know it's an old cliché, a well-used cover for infidelity, but I really was working late at the office.' His eyes burned into hers. 'You've got to believe me.'

Leah's stomach was grinding like a millstone inside her. 'Do you really mean that? Honestly? You're not lying?'

'Honestly. I'm not lying.' He smiled a fleeting smile and held her hands tightly as he continued, 'I have my faults, I know I'm far from perfect, but marriage is an institution I take very seriously. For a start, it would never even enter my mind to marry a woman I did not love, and neither would I ever be unfaithful to my wife.'

He looked deep into her eyes, frowning slightly. 'I told you a long time ago that fidelity was important to me. I told you I could not envisage a marriage without it.'

Leah's heart swelled inside her. She remembered that vividly. And she also remembered how she had assured him that, without reservation, she shared his beliefs.

As his eyes bored into hers, searching, probing, she was suddenly overcome with an urge to open up to him. Finally to unburden herself and confess the truth about her infidelity with the garage mechanic.

'Vincenzo...'

Heart thundering, she opened her mouth to speak. But even as the words formed in her mouth, a vision of Franca flashed into her head. Franca. His fiancée. The woman he was to marry. The woman he loved, as perhaps, once, he had loved her.

And in that instant she knew that what she'd been about to say to him was totally superfluous. It no longer mattered.

But he was waiting for her to continue. 'Yes, *cara*. Tell me.' Like endless pools of blackness, his eyes seemed to draw her.

She snatched her gaze away and heard herself saying in a voice that felt as though it belonged to someone else, 'I thought I'd better tell you, I'm not pregnant...'

'You're sure?'

'Quite sure. My period's started.' It had started that morning. She tried to pull her hands free. 'Lucky for both of us. Now we can just forget about the past and get on with the future—and that's what matters.' She looked into his face, her heart beating wildly. 'Let's hope that both of us have learned our lessons and will make a better job of our relationships in the future.' She forced a smile. 'I know I'm determined to. I'm going to make a success of my marriage to Ronald.'

Still he held her hands lightly, making her flesh burn. He looked deep into her eyes. 'This Ronald of yours... Are you sure that he's the right man for you?'

'Absolutely sure.' She struggled again to be free of him. 'He's a wonderful man. Just what I need.'

'I hope you're right.' His tone was earnest. 'I would hate you to make a mistake a second time.' To her horror he reached out to touch her hair with his fingers. 'What happened between us was partly my fault. I should have taken greater care to let you know how much I loved you.' He smiled a rueful smile and let his fingers brush her cheek. 'I hope Ronald makes a better husband than I did. I reckon you deserve a bit of happiness.'

Leah's heart was breaking with emotion inside her. She could scarcely breathe. Her blood was pounding. And she was suddenly filled with an agonising need to fling herself into his arms and tell him the truth.

But at that very moment there was a knock on the door and Jo came walking into the room.

CHAPTER TWELVE

IMMEDIATELY, the attention of both switched to Jo. And it was Jo who spoke first, addressing Leah.

'I expected you to be alone.' She slanted a hostile look at Vincenzo. 'I had no idea you would have company.'

Vincenzo rose to his feet. 'I was just leaving,' he told her. He thrust his hands into his trouser pockets. 'Where's Carlo? Is he with you? Has something happened?'

'Nothing's happened.' Jo's tone was not friendly. 'He's gone to the flat off the Via del Corso. If you want to talk to him, that's where you'll find him.'

Vincenzo nodded. 'Fine. That's what I'll do.' Then he turned almost awkwardly towards Leah. 'Goodnight,' he bade her. 'And goodbye,' he added. 'I don't expect we'll be seeing each other again.'

Leah rose to her feet shakily. Her heart felt cold and empty. 'No, I don't expect so,' she answered. 'Goodbye, Vincenzo.'

He neither kissed her nor shook her hand in farewell, and, in spite of the deep sense of despair that possessed her, in a way Leah felt grateful for that omission. If he had touched her, she might have been tempted to cling to him and beg him not to leave her. And it was better like this. A clean simple parting. Yet her heart wrenched inside her as he strode towards the door.

One final glance like a knife driving through her. Then he was gone and the door had closed behind him.

'What was he doing here?' Jo's tone was hostile. 'He hasn't been upsetting you, has he?'

Leah took a deep breath and turned to face her sister. 'Don't worry, he hasn't been upsetting me. We were just having a little chat about private things.'

'Are you sure?' Jo squinted at Leah's pale face. 'You look upset. Are you sure you're OK?'

'Absolutely sure.' Leah forced a bright smile. 'Come and sit down. Would you like something to drink?' As she crossed to the fridge-bar, she forced herself to breathe slowly. It was a blessing, she assured herself, that Jo had come when she had. She'd been saved from making an absolute fool of herself.

She poured two fruit juices and handed one to Jo. 'I'm so pleased to see you. But why have you come?' She seated herself on the bed beside her sister. 'You are all right, aren't you? Nothing's wrong?'

Jo took the glass she offered. 'Yes, I'm fine... Just riddled with guilt about the way I behaved the other day.' She grimaced and laid one hand softly on Leah's arm. 'I behaved like a child, and so did Carlo. I know you were only doing what you did because you care for me.'

Leah smiled. 'I'm glad you realise it.' And she clasped her hand in Jo's as her sister hurried on,

'I'm sorry for putting you through all of this. It must have been awful for you having to get mixed up again with Vincenzo.' She sighed. 'I could see the pain in your face when you said that stuff at the very end about not wanting to see me get destroyed as you were.' She squeezed Leah's hand. 'I've been very selfish, and I think it's time I put you in the picture.'

Leah swallowed hard at the mention of Vincenzo, and felt a rush of shame at her sister's observation. Had her pain that day really been so obvious?

She kept her voice steady. 'OK. I'm listening.'

'Right. This is the story.' Jo took a mouthful of her orange juice and leaned back on one elbow against the coverlet. 'When I came to Rome, I was following in your footsteps. It's a period of your life I've always been curious about. Then, when I met Carlo—quite by accident, at a disco—I was drawn to him, partly out of curiosity, but mainly because I happen to rather like him.' She paused. 'I may even be a tiny bit in love with him.' She held Leah's eye. 'But I do not intend to marry him.'

For some quite incomprehensible reason, Leah failed to feel the huge relief she'd expected. She said, 'I see. Then why were you thinking about staying on in Rome and giving up your studies back home?'

'Mainly for the experience of living in another country, finding out how other people live. But it was never my intention to give up my studies, only to delay them for a year.' Jo crossed her jeans-clad legs and smiled. 'But I've finally decided against that idea. I'll be going back home in a couple of weeks and starting my degree course exactly as planned.'

'And what about Carlo?'

'We'll remain friends. I hope in the future I'll see him again.' Then she made a face. 'I would've told you this before, but I really resented it when you started coming on heavy and telling me what

I ought to be doing with my life. That was why I let you go on believing that the whole thing was more serious than it really was.

'But then, as I said, that episode at the villa made me realise what I was putting you through.' She leaned towards Leah. 'I'm sorry, Sis. I was stupid. You were only thinking of my good.'

'Of course, I was. I love you, you dope.' With a lump in her throat, Leah pulled her towards her, wrapped her arms around her and gave her a hug.

And suddenly, she could no longer hold back the tears that had been aching inside her since Vincenzo walked out. As her sister hugged her warmly in return, they poured down her cheeks in a helpless burning flood.

After Jo had left, to rejoin Carlo and enjoy the rest of her Roman holiday, Leah picked up the phone and called down to Reception.

'I'll be leaving tomorrow,' she told the desk clerk. 'Please have my bill ready first thing in the morning.'

Then she climbed into bed. It was after one and she was exhausted. Every atom of her being was craving for sleep.

But sleep would not come. She lay in the darkness and tossed and turned and thought of Vincenzo.

And the more she thought of him and of what he had told her, the more helpless with misery she became. She had thrown away her marriage over a misunderstanding. She had ruined her life for a hurt that had never been.

For she believed his explanation of that over-heard conversation. She could remember him complaining about those problems with the Ministry.

And she realised now that only her own insecurities had led her to that fatal misinterpretation. She had simply believed the thing she had feared most.

She clenched her fists and pressed her face against the pillows, the pain inside her so fierce that she thought it must devour her. It had been bad enough to lose him, believing he had never loved her. At least she could console herself that the marriage was better dead. But to know that she was the one who had killed it needlessly, when, all the time, he had loved her and been her faithful husband...that was more than her heart could bear.

She could see his face as he told her that he'd loved her, that he would never have dreamed of marrying her otherwise, and she could feel again, too, that compulsion that had gripped her to throw herself into his arms and confess all her lies.

The lie about Ronald. That he was not her fiancé. That he had never been and would never be more than a friend.

And that other lie, the one she had used to gain her freedom, that freedom that now she reviled with all her heart. For there had been no affair with that Romeo car mechanic. She had simply made Vincenzo believe it so that he would allow her to leave.

Tears streamed from her eyes. How she had longed to tell him. But she recognised all too cruelly the fear that had held her back.

He was no longer hers. He was soon to marry Franca. And she had known with a sense of shame and anguish that to have told him the truth would have been to beg his forgiveness and plead for a fresh chance for their marriage.

With courage she might have resisted putting the plea into words, but he would have seen it shining naked and raw in her eyes. He would have seen what she herself had only just realised. That she still loved him. Desperately. With all her heart.

And, seeing that, he would have pitied her, and his pity was something she knew she could not live with.

Miserably, she turned over and buried her face in her hands and prayed with all her strength for morning to come. The sooner she was gone from here, the sooner she could begin to pick up the pieces of her bruised and broken life.

Leah was up early and on the phone to the airport immediately to book herself a seat on the first available flight to London.

Then, ignoring breakfast—she couldn't have eaten—she was throwing her things haphazardly into her bags and getting ready to meet the taxi she had ordered. It would get her to the airport far too early, but she would sooner wait there than hang around at the hotel. At the airport she would feel that her journey had started. That Rome and Vincenzo were already behind her.

She stifled the thought. She mustn't think of Vincenzo. To think of Vincenzo would only break her heart. He was the only man she had ever loved. Or ever could love, come to that. And, out of fear and foolishness, she had lost him. She had even taught him to hate and despise her.

Poor fool that I am. She snapped shut her suitcase and pulled on the jacket of her blue cotton two-piece. To have thrown away such a man, who loved me, because I was too fearful and immature to accept his love. And then for five foolish years to have pretended that I hated him when I could never hate him. What a child I've been.

As she started to leave the room, she glanced at her reflection. A child no more, eyes clouded with wisdom. Now the answer to her pain was neither love nor hate. The only thing that could save her was forgetfulness, God's most merciful gift to mankind.

Down in Reception Leah handed in her key—the bill she had already settled earlier—and was told by the receptionist, 'Your taxi's just arrived, miss.' With a wave he summoned the elderly cab driver who'd been waiting inconspicuously in a corner of the lobby. 'Shall I call a porter to carry your bags to the car?'

'Thank you.' Leah nodded and began to follow the cab driver across the lobby to the main door of the hotel—when at that very moment, with the suddenness of a whirlwind, Franca came bursting through the door.

'Thank heavens I caught you!' She rushed up to Leah and caught her firmly by the arm. Her eyes in her flushed face were bright and anxious. 'I have to speak to you. It's very important.'

'Vincenzo?' The fear that something had happened to him was the very first thought that lurched into Leah's head.

'Yes, it's about Vincenzo that I want to talk to you. But, don't worry, he's safe. Nothing's happened to him.'

Thank heaven for that! Leah frowned at Franca. 'So why have you come here? Why do you want to see me?'

'I have something to tell you.' She glanced at the cab driver. 'Are you on your way to the airport? OK, I'm coming with you. There's something you must know before you get on that plane.'

A moment later she was propelling a bewildered Leah into the back seat of the cab, then turning towards her, her expression earnest. 'I want you to listen very carefully to what I have to say to you.'

Twenty minutes later, when she had finally finished speaking and they were rapidly approaching Leonardo da Vinci airport, Leah leaned forward suddenly to address the cab driver.

'I've changed my mind. I'm not going to the airport. Take me to the Petruzzi Automobili test-track instead.'

Franca kissed her delightedly. 'Good girl, Leah! That's precisely what I was praying you'd do.'

The journey to the test-track seemed to take for ever, yet when at last they drew up outside the main gates Leah was suddenly so filled with anxiety that she barely had the strength to climb out of the cab. Her brain was buzzing with what Franca had just told her. Her heart was beating so hard that she felt it must explode.

But next moment, in a kind of daze, she was walking on firm strides through the gates, with Franca following close behind her.

'I'll take you to the edge of the track,' she had told her. 'The place has changed a lot. You may not find your way.'

Then she was being led past a line of brand new offices and the more familiar sprawling array of works buildings to the very edge of the smoky, dusty test-track. And instantly she felt her heart swell inside her as she caught sight of Vincenzo, in white mechanic's overalls, stepping out of one of the cars.

'OK, it's all yours now.'

Franca drew discreetly back, as, on legs that had suddenly turned to rubber, Leah headed towards the overalls-clad figure, fists clenched tightly at her sides, apprehension and excitement beating inside her.

The things she had just been told were a revelation. But was it really possible that all of them were true?

A few feet away from the waist-high barrier that circled the edge of the dusty test-track, she raised one arm nervously to attract his attention.

'Vincenzo!' she called, her voice sounding croaky. She cleared her throat. 'Vincenzo!' she called again.

He turned round instantly, and as his eyes fell on her, the shadow of a frown seemed to darken his face, very nearly causing her to lose her nerve. Just for an instant she was tempted to turn tail. Then she saw his gaze drift past her to where Franca was standing, and a moment later, after only the tiniest of pauses, he had vaulted the barrier and was heading towards her.

It's Franca he's coming to see, Leah thought in sudden anguish. But as she glanced round swiftly to where Franca had been, she caught sight of her striding off towards the office buildings. When she turned back Vincenzo was standing just a few feet away.

For a moment that seemed an eternity he simply looked at her. Then in a flat voice he observed, 'This is a turn-up for the books.'

'I hope I'm not interrupting?' Where could she begin? There was suddenly so much she wanted to say to him. As he shook his head, she smiled at him awkwardly. 'Franca said you'd come here to drown your sorrows. She said you always come here when you're upset about something.'

His eyes were on her face, but she could not read them. His expression was shuttered, giving nothing away. She felt a flutter of panic. Had Franca been mistaken?

He took a deep breath. 'Yes, I find driving therapeutic. I often come here when things are going wrong.'

The words gave her heart a lift. She swallowed hard, aware that her tightly clenched fists felt clammy. 'I've just had a long chat with Franca,' she told him. 'She told me a lot of very interesting things.'

His expression barely altered. 'Like what, for example?'

Leah took a deep breath. 'Like that you and she are not engaged.'

His reaction was much the same as Franca's had been when Leah had revealed to her in the cab that she had believed that she and Vincenzo were affianced. 'Engaged? Are you crazy? Franca and I are friends! Whatever gave you the idea that we were engaged?'

Leah pulled a face. 'It's an old habit of mine. I put two and two together and keep coming up with five.' She kept her eyes on his face. 'She came to the hotel to tell me that you weren't lovers. She said she had suddenly realised that that was what I was thinking and she wanted to put me straight in case...'

A ROMAN MARRIAGE

183

As her voice trailed off, Vincenzo's dark eyes narrowed. 'In case?' he queried. Then he went on before she could answer, 'I wondered myself if that was what you were thinking. You more or less said it a couple of times. But it seemed so preposterous...' He paused and shook his head. 'Anyway, in the circumstances, it hardly seemed worth explaining. After all, it wouldn't have changed anything.'

Oh, but it would! Her heart was beating wildly. 'If I hadn't believed that you were lovers...engaged...I would never have invented a fiancé of my own.' She pushed back her hair with nervous fingers. 'I made all that up. I have no fiancé.'

That stopped him short. 'What about Ronald?' A strange expression had crept into his face.

'Ronald's just a friend. Purely platonic. I have no serious boyfriend. I never have had.'

'You mean that?'

Leah nodded.

He shook his head in silence. Then he stepped towards her. 'Thank God,' he whispered.

His hands were on her shoulders, lightly holding her. His eyes, as black as midnight, blazed down into hers. He said in a low voice, 'What I told you last night...about that conversation with Piero that you overheard... You do believe me, don't you, Leah?'

Leah nodded. 'I believe you.' Her breath shuddered within her. 'I only wish I'd known the truth about that years ago.'

'I wish you had, too.' He drew her towards him. 'But now at least I understand why you were so anxious to leave me all these years ago.'

So anxious she had been prepared to adopt any methods, even the fatal blackening of her own reputation. She opened her mouth now to reveal that painful lie, but, before she could speak, he was drawing her closer and tilting her chin to look down into her face.

'I've never stopped loving you, Leah,' he was saying. 'I've never stopped wishing that I could have you back...' As he paused, his eyes black fire, she could feel his heart beating. '*Sposa mia,* will you stay with me? Please?'

Tears sprang to her eyes. For a moment she could not answer. Her heart filled to overflowing, she pressed against him. Then, as he kissed her hair, she raised her eyes to his.

'Forever!' she whispered. 'Forever, my love!'

Then he was gathering her almost fiercely into his arms, covering her face with sweet, burning kisses. 'I love you, *sposa mia*! How much I love you! The past five years have been hell without you. That was why I didn't want the divorce. I kept hoping something would happen to bring you back to me.'

'I was hoping the same.' She realised that now. The thought of divorce had secretly appalled her. 'But why did you tell me that you wanted one now?'

He shook his head. 'Madness. To provoke a re-action. I was praying you would say you didn't agree.'

'Oh, darling, Vincenzo...' She leaned against him, but, as he kissed her again, she caught her breath and told him,

'There's still something rather important I have to tell you.'

When she had finished with her revelation, there was a moment of silence. Vincenzo's eyes looked down at her, dark and endless.

'You mean you were never unfaithful to me with that man? That the entire story was an invention?'

Leah nodded, shame-faced. 'It was the only solution. Unless you thought I'd been unfaithful, I knew, you'd never let me go.'

'I should have stopped you anyway.' His voice was ragged with emotion. 'I shouldn't have allowed my pride to dictate to me.'

'But you couldn't have stopped me. I'd have found some other way. Believing you didn't love me, there was no way I would have stayed.'

She reached up to kiss his lips. 'But you can take my word for it, in all these five years I've never been unfaithful to you. Neither in thought nor in deed. I was never even tempted.'

'I don't deserve that.' He kissed her softly. Then, with a smile, he glanced round at their less than private surroundings. 'What do you say we go back to the villa, take the phone off the hook and bolt all the doors? I think we've a little bit of catching up to do.'

Leah felt her stomach curl with delicious anticipation. 'I can't think of a nicer idea,' she assured him. She looked deep into his eyes. 'I love you, Vincenzo.'

'And I love you.' He took her hand and kissed her fingers, then slid one arm around her waist and proceeded to lead her to his car.

'Come, *sposa mia*. Let me show you just how much.'

* * *

The villa was filled with the perfume of flowers—the huge bouquet that Jo and Carlo had sent to congratulate the happy couple on their reconciliation, and the even more enormous bouquet from Franca.

'I couldn't be happier,' she had told a beaming Leah when she had phoned her at the villa just a couple of days ago. 'I always sensed that you and Vincenzo would get back together. I knew how much he loved you, so you had to be pretty special to keep a man like that carrying a torch for so long.'

She had paused and confided, 'And then when I met you I instantly sensed that you loved him, too, but that for some reason you were trying to smother your love.' Then she had laughed. 'I do hope that now everything's been resolved you and I are going to be friends?'

'I just know we are!' Leah meant it. Hadn't she always felt a grudging liking for Franca? It was only her jealousy that had got in the way. 'If it hadn't been for you, we might never have got back together. Both of us will always be eternally grateful.'

Nothing could be truer. They owed a double debt to Franca.

'It was largely thanks to Franca's cajoling that I changed my mind about taking you to Paluro,' Vincenzo had revealed soon after their reconciliation. 'If you remember, she rang just after your outburst at the villa and it suddenly struck me that perhaps, after all, it was worth the two of us spending time together. I knew I still loved you and you obviously still felt something.'

Leah had kissed him. 'I always wondered about that. It isn't like you to change your mind.'

He had hugged her to him. 'Thank heaven I did. But one thing I know I'll never change my mind about is the way I feel for you.'

Leah paused now to glance around the splendid dining-room, all decked out for the evening's dinner party, making a swift check of the silver and gleaming crystal on the table.

'Everything in order?'

At the sound of Vincenzo's voice she spun round to see him standing in the doorway. And as always her heart leapt at the sight of him. That tall, commanding figure, dressed formally now in a dark suit, that dark-eyed, handsome, deeply adored face.

'Everything in order,' she assured him, smiling. 'Including the host, I'm pleased to see.'

He came towards her. 'You're looking beautiful.' His eyes drifted over the aquamarine silk dress with its tiny cinched-in waist and elegantly dropped shoulders. 'But then, *sposa mia,* you are always beautiful. The most beautiful woman in the world.'

Leah flushed with pleasure as he leaned to kiss her. 'I hope you're not going to make passes in front of our guests,' she teased.

'Do you think they'd be shocked?'

'Actually, I think they'd be pleased.' After all, their intimate quartet of guests—Jo and Carlo and Franca and Luigi—the man who was Franca's legitimate fiancé!—were among those who had been most delighted by the reunion.

'In that case I shall make passes and flirt with you all night. It is the duty of a host to please his guests.'

Leah laughed happily. 'You're impossible!' And as she looked into his eyes she was sharply conscious of the sense of deep contentment that had flowered within her. The past few days had been filled with love and laughter, heart-to-heart talks that went on long into the night, plans for the future, five years of catching up.

And the bond between them was stronger now than ever. So strong that she knew no power on earth could break it.

Vincenzo kissed her face. 'I almost forgot to tell you... That chap from Tessuti Moderni phoned while you were out to say they were extremely interested in hiring you.' He smiled. 'At this rate, you'll have every fabric design company in Italy fighting to offer you a job.'

Leah smiled smugly. 'They seem to recognise talent.' Then she laughed as Vincenzo poked her playfully in the ribs. And, inwardly she felt a surge of gratitude that the company who had previously employed her in London had generously agreed to let her leave without notice on condition that she finish on a freelance basis the designs she'd been working on before she went on holiday. She had been spared the separation from Vincenzo that she'd feared.

He seemed to read her thoughts. 'So, how does it feel to be back? Back at the Villa Petruzzi where you belong?'

She smiled at him. 'It feels as though I've never been away. Perhaps in my heart I never really left.'

'And you never shall again.' He pulled her to him. 'From now on, where I am is where you will be, too.' He looked into her eyes. 'Is that agreed, *sposa mia*?'

Leah nodded. 'That is all in the world that I wish.'

Vincenzo kissed her. 'Then, my love, it is yours.'

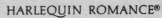
HARLEQUIN ROMANCE®

**Harlequin Romance
makes love
an adventure!**

Don't miss
next month's
exciting story in

THE BRIDAL COLLECTION

RESCUED BY LOVE
by Anne Marie Duquette

THE BRIDE wanted a new future.
THE GROOM was haunted by his past.
THEIR WEDDING was a Grand affair!

Available this month in
The Bridal Collection:
A BRIDE FOR RANSOM
by Renee Roszel
Harlequin Romance #3251
Wherever Harlequin books are sold.

WED-11

Where do you find hot Texas nights, smooth Texas charm and dangerously sexy cowboys?

Crystal Creek

DEEP IN THE HEART

Wedding Bells—Texas Style!

Even a Boston blue blood needs a Texas education. Ranch owner J. T. McKinney is handsome, strong, opinionated and totally charming. And he is determined to marry beautiful Bostonian Cynthia Page. However, the couple soon discovers a Texas cattleman's idea of marriage differs greatly from a New England career woman's!

CRYSTAL CREEK reverberates with the exciting rhythm of Texas. Each story features the rugged individuals who live and love in the Lone Star State. And each one ends with the same invitation...

Y'ALL COME BACK...REAL SOON!

Don't miss *DEEP IN THE HEART* by Barbara Kaye. Available in March wherever Harlequin books are sold.

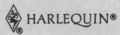

The most romantic day of the year is here! Escape into the exquisite world of love with MY VALENTINE 1993. What better way to celebrate Valentine's Day than with this very romantic, sensuous collection of four original short stories, written by some of Harlequin's most popular authors.

**ANNE STUART
JUDITH ARNOLD
ANNE McALLISTER
LINDA RANDALL WISDOM**

**THIS VALENTINE'S DAY, DISCOVER ROMANCE
WITH MY VALENTINE 1993**

Available in February wherever Harlequin Books are sold. VAL93